# Eternal and Boundless

## by

## Jesus Misfits

Published by Jesusmisfits.com

Printed by Book Printing UK www.bookprintinguk.com

Remus House, Coltsfoot Drive, Peterborough, PE2 9BF


Printed in Great Britain

ISBN  978-1-3999-7552-0

First Edition 2024

Jesus Misfits

Jesusmisfits.com

# Contents

# 1

# The short man

Bea watched her corpse-like body on the bed. *I'm not moving, but breathing. I look like a dead 12-year-old but, according to the monitor, I'm alive.* Bea was pleased with her quick medical assessment. Her body had a blue bruise, the size of a football, covering her right forearm. She noted the purple bruise on the right side of her brow next to a slim bandage on her head. *I don't seem to be that damaged. This is better than looking in a mirror, because I can see myself from any angle.* She looked at her body from her feet's perspective and from both sides. *I seem fatter now I'm outside of my body. It's not because I don't eat vegetables, or anything that might have a sneaky vegetable, or anything green, like kiwi, which is hairy anyway.* In fact, Bea didn't even eat green sweets, to be on the safe side. *Hospitals make you fat, it's all the lying down.* Bea wasn't totally sure she had convinced herself. She chewed her pyjama sleeve thoughtfully. She had never doubted that she was right before; she always knew she was.

Bea grew bored of her body; it wasn't waking up. It was connected to a high-tech monitor which displayed a whole range of data at once and, reassuringly, beeped. A sticker on the monitor read "Leicester Victoria Children's Hospital". She pottered around the room. It was in the oldest part of the hospital, saddened by overpainted copper pipes and pale green walls. There was a board separating her cubicle from another patient on the other side. *I won't peek in, they may be awake, and start talking.* She backed away at the thought of it and looked out of the window. It was just getting light. A man was pushing a laundry trolley over the cobbles below. The odd patter of nurse's feet clipped the corridor behind her door.

She felt grumpy; grumpy was her go-to emotion. *Grumpy is safe, No one upsets you when you're already grumpy.* Bea had practised a lifetime of grumpy and had perfected her scowl. *Why am I not inside my body? Why is it acting like a limp fish floating on the top* of the fish tank? Why isn't Mum here? She should be; I'm in hospital. Why are my thoughts so much easier to express outside my body?

As if in answer, a man in a hat lurched out of the sickly green wall. He wore a thin, dark suit that was too small for him with a thin, grey tie. His bowler hat squeezed in at the bottom as if it was struggling to stay on his head without a firmer grip, and his sunglasses didn't seem to keep the sun out, but the light in. He was practically the same height as Bea and, considering she was tall for 12, that made him small. His torso jolted back as he examined the situation and he disappeared. *He's a bit early.* Bea, surprised herself that she understood the weird little man's body language. *How did he get in the wall?*

Before she had time to process the stranger, a nurse swung through the door, guiding her weeping mother into her cubicle. *So, you finally show up and as usual you're focused on yourself! No thought for me and my body in the bed and myself over here! Any opportunity to get some sympathy!* The nurse passed her mum some tissues and checked the monitor.

"Mum! Stop crying for yourself! And look at me, I'm in two places! Look at me!" she tugged at her mum's jumper furiously. It made no difference; her mum didn't hear, see or feel her and neither did the nurse. "Mum! stop feeling sorry for yourself and focus on me! I'm disconnected!" she shouted. "Argh!" She thumped the bed and then realised she might bruise her own body lying there, so she threw herself against the wall. Bea hated being ignored. "You selfish! Stupid! Horrible Mum! No wonder you've got no friends I hate you too!" she screamed through her clenched jaw.

The nurse held her mum tenderly as she sobbed.

"Argh!" yelled Bea in frustration. No one heard, so she gathered her thoughts. *Why is Mum crying?* Bea moaned. *It's not like she's in hospital? Unless she is crying because I'm dying? Or crying because the nurse said I'm getting better and I can go home soon and Mum is thinking of herself as usual! Yes! Probably! Or because I'm going to be in bed forever and she can't get the bed home because it won't fit in a taxi?* A thought shocked her: *What if I can never get back in my body! And it just lies there forever!*

The nurse approached the monitor. Bea gripped her Mum's arms. "Stop crying!" she warned. Bea squeezed the saggy pillow of flesh around her Mum's waist, but her mother couldn't feel Bea. Bea pinched her – no reaction. "Argh!" screeched Bea. Her mum lifted her hand to talk to the nurse and Bea bit it. No reaction at all.

Bea tried a demanding tone: "You're not the one dying! Stop it! Look at me!" Bea was shocked – her voice sounded different, definite, more expressive and real. *Am I dying? Is that why I sound different?*

"Everything is normal," said the nurse, continuing her conversation with her mum.

Bea turned to the nurse "Really?"

The nurse continued, oblivious: "She could be like this for a long time."

"No," said Bea. "No way! No, I won't!"

"A coma can be a long-term process, so you need to look after yourself and get some rest," the nurse advised her mother gently.

Her mum nodded as she accepted the situation, still sniffling into her tissue.

"Oh yes! You get to look after you! You'll like that! Go book yourself on a holiday, like you always wanted! You get yourself some rest! That's all you talk about, you and your need for a break! You're selfish!" Bea coaxed her anger towards it's crescendo "You don't care! You never cared! You hate me! I know you do! I hate you! You're not my mum!" Bea crumpled to the floor, besides herself with grief at her loss of power to change anything.

"We'll ring if anything alters," explained the nurse.

"No! No! No! Don't you go!" Bea shouted. As the feelings of loss and powerlessness began to roll over her, she threw her head back on the floor, banging it against the coldness, hoping the impact would bring release. There was no sting of pain. Bea let herself sweep into the engulfing rage. She tried to throw a pillow, but her body was lying on it.

Her mum gathered her things together and wiped her mascara smudges. She looked at Bea's body in the bed. "She looks so peaceful," her mum sighed.

Bea thumped the hard, slightly rivety non-slip floor with her fists, again and again. There was nothing: no sensation, no release.

"I'll be back later," her mum said, kissing Bea's body gently on the cheek.

Bea grabbed her mum's legs to stop her leaving, tears rolling down her face. Bea wailed "No! No! Don't go! Mummy! Don't leave me!"

Her mum walked effortlessly around the bed and out the door, and the nurse followed her out.

Bea lay on her back wailing, and when that didn't help, she lay on her front and thumped her fists on the bobbly, irritating surface. Finally, she lay in a curled-up ball on her side and sobbed a little. The room went quiet.

"Traitor," Bea said under her breath. Then she checked herself and said it again: "Traitor." It was a bit of a surprise, so she sat up and wiped the snot around her cheeks a little more with her hand and thought about it. She couldn't remember ever knowing the word or ever speaking it, but now it was there, and she knew what it meant. "Traitor," she said, emphasising its meaning with a squint of her eyes.

"Interesting word," said the little man in the hat staring at her from behind his dark glasses.

*He's back.* Bea pretended to ignore him and wiped her nose and tears on the duvet cover hanging from the bed. *He is bound to go in a minute.* She stared intently at the duvet. *Nope, he's still here. Another minute, then.*

"Bea," said the stranger, not moving from his original position, and keeping still, as if he had spotted a stray dog and didn't want to scare it off. "Bea. Do you know why you're not in your body?"

"No," said Bea, sitting up and examining her sock. *I may not have my body but I'm still in my socks.* She waited for the visitor's explanation. When he didn't give her one. She stretched her neck and peeked over the bed.

"Bea, you've been given time out of your body to find something that you need; when you receive it, you can go back to your body." The sightseer spoke slowly, allowing her to focus on the words.

"I need my mum," said Bea, checking her PJs carefully for any wet spots.

"Your mum will be by your bed when you're back in your body." He was waiting for this to sink in. His hands were pressed to his sides so the movement didn't confuse the stressed creature. "Obtain what you're missing and it will help you to return to your body." He sounded like a teacher. Her teacher, Miss Cotton, spoke slowly and carefully to her at times. Teachers were safe, but only wore hats on spelling day. He didn't have a word on his hat.

"Are you a teacher?" she asked without looking.

"I am the great life teacher," said the teacher. "I can teach you everything about life."

"Is it quick?" said Bea.

"It's fun," he replied.

*Nothing you learn is that much fun*, thought Bea.

The teacher bent forward slightly. "Do you think you've been really living?"

"Well, I was alive and I was in my body," said Bea, listening to the sound of her voice and being rather pleased with its new clarity.

"But were you living?" the teacher impressed "What if you could be more?" The end of his tie lifted up and waved at her.

Bea did not like clown tricks, but she wanted to study the stranger. She pulled herself upright and checked out his feet; he had pointed shoes with tiny holes imprinted on the leather at the front.

"Why do your shoes have holes?" The teacher was surprised at the question. She glanced up at his face and clocked his surprise.

She was annoyed at his questions, his persistence and his surprise.

*What are you hiding behind those sunglasses?* She lunged to pull them off his face. At the same moment, he disappeared. The momentum was overwhelming, she tripped and landed on the wall, only it wasn't there, and she was in a corridor. She looked around, trying to get her bearings, but there weren't any, just a completely empty hospital corridor and the teacher. He was 15 metres away, perched on a pink, push-along scooter. His tie was firmly back in his jacket.

"Is that mine?" she asked.

"Could be," he replied defiantly, scooting it backwards and forwards, to get the feel of it.

"Give it back!" she said.

"Didn't yours break a few years ago?" He raised an eyebrow.

"Give it back ..."

Bea stopped to picture a vivid memory, clearly and in colour; it was a weird and unusual experience. She saw her pink scooter lying partially on her drive and the remnants of her wheel in a red flowering bush with dark green leaves. "Wow, I can see that!"

"Good," the teacher assessed, before introducing the next subject. "Your body is in hospital. Do you remember?"

She visualised her body on the bed, and focused on the detailed monitor next to it. "Yes," she replied. *That's so strange. I can almost touch it, it's so clear.*

"Good," said the man, as if measuring her imagination. "Your school bus crashed." He scooted forwards a few metres.

Bea, waited for the imagery. She visualised the bus and the driver. She was staring out of the bus window, exploring her distorted reflection in the glass. A car with two men in it overtook the bus. Then nothing.

"I can't see that," she said.

"You're in a coma," he continued, scooting forwards again.

She easily visualised the nurse explaining this to her mum, "Well, my body is."

"You are having a reaction to the coma."

"How do you know?" asked Bea, getting tired of the conversation.

"I know all things." He lifted the scooter on its two back wheels and balanced it perfectly. He expected applause but didn't get any. Bea was processing all of this.

"Are you Death?" said Bea.

"No," said the little man, unsurprised at the deduction. "A good guess. Do you normally guess?"

"Only when I can't be bothered to pick an answer," she replied truthfully.

"I am Eternal. You don't have to die now; you have a choice," he explained helpfully. He scooted closer.

"I chose to live in my body. Are you Death?" she repeated.

"Eternal, by name and nature," said Eternal. He was an arm's length away.

"That's your name? Eternal? And what you are?" Bea asked and understood at the same moment.

"I'm not a bee; I'm spelt with an 'a'," Bea explained.

"Yes," said Eternal, a little confused at the direction of the conversation. "And you've no wings."

"They got plucked off."

"But you're not a bee," said Eternal, sounding confused.

"No," said Bea, sighing and wishing she was, so she could buzz off.

"We are here because ..." Eternal added, in the hope of regaining ground.

"Bee – cause. That's a joke. Ha ha! That's a joke. I get it! I get it! Beeeeee-cause! Beeee-cause." She was delighted.

"It's a pun," Eternal sighed.

"What's happened to my brain? It's thinking differently?"

"Is it faster? Easier? More responsive?" he asked.

"I don't know. It's free! Free from my body."

"Do you prefer the freedom?" Eternal asked, examining her reaction to the change.

Bea was tired, "You said I have to find something to help me live in my body?"

"Exactly," said Eternal, obviously delighted at Bea's now rational thinking.

"What thing?"

"Excellent!" Eternal rubbed his hands in anticipation.

"Excellence?" quizzed Bea.

"No," snapped Eternal, desperate to keep to the point. "You need to find your destiny? Do you know what that is?"

"If I knew what it was, I wouldn't need to find it!" Bea retorted.

Eternal's hat twisted round on top of his head all by itself as he thought.

"You know everything, but you don't know me?" she asked.

"You are an exciting challenge, different," he explained. Eternal touched the rim and the hat stopped. He tried a different approach: "You have a purpose, which will give you a long life. I can show you your purpose ... and you want to live, don't you?"

"I don't know. What are the alternatives?" Bea was returning to grumpy. *I don't want to be your challenge! Or mum's challenge! Or my teacher's! Or my nan's! Or the doctor's or dentists! Or anybody else's! Why does everyone see me as a challenge!* "I'll find it myself," Bea muttered.

Eternal was getting out of his depth, and they were deep. He paused for a moment and readjusted his stance with one foot on the floor. He was losing engagement; this was serious. If she didn't re-engage, she could be lost, and he'd already lost one child.

"Okay," said Eternal, unexpectedly. "You can find it yourself." He paused to let her reconsider. "But it's a game and there are rules."

Bea showed no interest; she was still disconnecting.

"You have to break the rules," Eternal blurted out.

Bea re-engaged.

"Each rule you break takes you towards your destiny."

Bea refocused. "I get to break the rules," she smiled. "Won't that be dangerous?"

"You're in a hospital bed in a coma. You're totally safe. What's the worst that can happen?"

Bea thought for a moment. *Yes, I am safely in bed, I don't have anything else to do, what's the worst that can happen, really?*

Eternal described the perimeters of the game, by adding, "You can break nine universal rules. Each rule you break takes you further towards your destiny."

"What are the rules?" said Bea, fascinated by the new game.

"Ah! You're very clever, Bea; you can work them out. Once you have broken the ninth rule you will understand your destiny and be returned to your body to wake up."

Bea had never been described as clever: stupid, dumb, self-willed, grumpy, stubborn and obstinate were the main descriptions. *Why would he call me clever?*

Eternal was waiting, watching her think.

Bea wasn't thinking much. *I have to get back to my body somehow.* She wanted to rip Eternal's glasses off his face, because there was a light behind them and it was annoying her. He must have been reading her thoughts, because he flicked his sunglasses off to reveal fragments of black that shook in an empty space, shedding light at the back of his eye sockets. *He's not real. But I need to be back in my body.*

"So, are you ready to do this?" Eternal pushed, and the scooter slid away to the far end of the corridor.

Bea went into her starter's race pose, which wasn't too impressive, as she wasn't much of an athlete. She gave a deep breath out. "Ready!" Eternal revved the pink scooter from the other end of the corridor. With great determination she started running towards Eternal. He picked up speed on the pink scooter. She barely had time to consider the impact and had definitely not thought through consequences, but it felt at that moment as if there was only the corridor and little alternative.

Then, there she was, drawn out of the world, the darkness of space, the length of time, into the universe. The answers to life flashed before her briefly and were immediately forgotten. She'd left her body behind and felt as if, for the first time, she was free to really enjoy life.

# 2

# Gravity

Bea was still running, when she recognised the strip lighting. *One minute I'm floating through the universe, outside of everything and I think I'm on the edge of this huge understanding of something really life-changing, next moment back to the nothingness of life.* She tried to gauge her surroundings without slowing down. She was in an old, run-down part of the hospital. Disappointed, she slackened to a walk down a yellowing corridor. She tried to picture the cosmos, reliving the feeling, but it had evaporated. *What does it matter? Why would I have a destiny? Who'd care? He lied. Everyone lies. He said it was fun!* "Liar," she muttered out loud.

She stood still. The corridor lay behind her with its smell of disinfectant and stale food. Ahead was a door with a "Staff Only" sign. No one was about, so she tried the well-worn handle tentatively and the door opened. *There's no point heading back to the ward to gawp at my body; it's not like it's going anywhere. I might as well take a peek.* She struggled to adjust her eyes to the gloom inside. She heard the metal stairs under her feet and readjusted her balance. She tapped carefully down each step.

The air was stale and smelt of old people, a second-hand shop smell, but more pungent, and it lay in her mouth, like old teeth. An extraordinary heaviness enveloped her, making moving hard work. *I guess I imagined it. That silly little man is just a movie scene from my head. What movie? I dunno, I can't remember them all.* She remembered grey days when she'd not really done anything except watch movies and play games that just went on and on. *Just one more level, just one more. It's safer being in a game. Safer being in bed. Safer scrolling the internet. Was I living? Was I just being safe? What if that's all the living I get? And I spent it being safe?* The question made her feel uncomfortable, like a pair of dirty knickers that you hide in your drawer and hope will disappear.

She sat on the bottom metal step feeling small and alone. *I wonder if mum is back to visit me yet?* She was in a huge warehouse basement. It was massive, as if the whole hospital sat on top of it. Sunlight was seeping through the edges of the warehouse sliding doors, but there were no windows.

She headed for the light. An old, dirty table and chairs sat in front of the sliding doors. On it was an ashtray with cigarette ends, three mugs, a flask and a half-eaten packet of biscuits. It was so quiet and musty, like tiptoeing on someone's grave.

She peered through the gloomy greyness and recognised the outline of an enormous mountain of mattresses heaped up, under the stairs. The mattresses breathed. Nothing registered in her brain. They breathed again. Her brain clicked in: "You cannot breathe," she informed them.

"You're not real, so stop pretending," she sighed. *Why bother? Nothing is real, I'm not even real! My realness is upstairs lying on a bed. What am I waiting for? What am I searching for?* The mattresses were dirty and the smell pungent. Overwhelmed with tiredness, Bea checked out the mattresses. *They're disgusting. That one's got blood on it. I think that's poo. There's definitely wee.* She was still considering a sleep when the wallpaper distracted her.

As if designed for large warehouses, the wallpaper was in enormous strips and peeling off. *Well that's ridiculous, why bother to wallpaper an old hospital basement? Nothing else is wallpapered? It's not like people come down here.* She climbed onto a mattress and smoothed down some of the peeled paper. The wallpaper depicted an American GI facing her. He was about her size, his gun pointed at her head. He was bent over and creeping forward, as if she was the enemy. "Well, I'm not," she whispered. *What are the Americans doing in Leicester Victoria Children's Hospital?*

Further along the wall, behind the mattresses, was a small stack of war memorabilia, including some papers and a helmet and some uniforms. Behind that was an unused, unseen door. *What's through that door? I'll just take a little peek.* The thought itched at her, as Bea scrambled up the stuffy mattresses. They were slippery and lumpy and stacked like slides, so she held the sides to clamber further up. She scaled some and crawled up others. A couple of minutes later, she realised she wasn't getting to the top. She paused to consider this and felt the pad under her slip, it slid down like a toboggan to the bottom with Bea clinging on. *Woah! No way! Now I stink too ugh!*

Bea groaned. The mattress sighed back. *You're not alive! But I'll just check.* Bea did a little wiggle to see if the mattresses would wiggle. They didn't. *See I knew you weren't.* She began to ascend again. As she mounted her third mattress, she shot a look behind her. A stripy blue mattress sheepishly disappeared underneath the one above it. The mattresses had formed an escalator and she was going up the wrong way. *Oh no you don't, I'm quicker than you!* She crawled up the mattresses faster, but when she turned around, she was still no higher; the grey shiny mattress at the bottom slipped underneath a rotten old blue mattress and again she was sliding down.

"Very funny!" she shouted to the mattresses and tried to bolt to the top, but the mountain was far too steep and she slipped on a shiny mattress and slithered to the bottom on her belly like a starfish on a wet rock.

*Why is nothing easy? I can't even get up some old beds! Argh ... breathe, breathe.*

Bea stopped and analysed the opponent. *There must be a way round them.* She walked nonchalantly towards the stairs; the mattresses regrouped like rugby players preparing for the next scrum. *I don't want to get through the door, I'm just having a potter about, round here, like this.* She ran full pelt at the mattresses from the other side and tried to clamber around them. The smell of hospital sickness and mustiness puffed out of each one she jumped on. The slippery plastic coatings slid her feet downwards. She pressed for the top and knew she'd reached it, only to turn around and find herself three mattresses up and sliding again towards the floor.

"This isn't funny! Stop it." She kicked the nearest mattress. As an afterthought, she commanded them: "Stand still! I need to get to the door." The mattresses seemed to understand and settled themselves down. "Thank you," she said, and put her foot on the first mattress. It slipped shyly under the mattress above it, leaving her foot in thin air.

"Argh!" shouted Bea, rotating a full circle. She spotted the table and chair again and went to sit down with her arms folded, as if she wasn't bothered, hoping the mattresses would slide off. She peered round. They watched her. *The chair isn't dusty – whoever comes down here, comes regularly.* She was pleased with her analysis. *They shouldn't smoke in here; those mattresses will catch fire and the whole hospital will go up, and my body is still in that bed!*

Bea sneaked a look. The mattresses had regrouped around the door, aware of her goal, with just a right-hand corner of the door temptingly visible.

Bea focused on the wallpaper figure. *He isn't wearing the same outfit as my dad.* She visualised a photo of her dad in his American army uniform on her mum's phone. *How do I know it's an American soldier?*

Bea pulled at her mouth distractedly as she refocused on her dad. Dad had not stayed long with mum. He had left when she was little and moved back to America with a tart called Rachel, whose hair wasn't really red. She had considered this at length. *Rachel can't be described as a strawberry jam or raspberry tart as she isn't really red. So, she must be an apple tart, as they can be green and red.* She didn't eat any jam tarts, out of loyalty to her mum, and in case they had vegetables in. She felt reassured by the reality of her scatterbrain thoughts.

"Are you in a pickle?" asked a helpful voice, adjusting his sunglasses with one hand.

*Yes, but I'm not telling you.* "No," she lied to the superior being. *I'm not sure you're real or telling the truth, but if you're not real why would you lie? So, if you're lying you must be real? But what if you're telling the truth?* She avoided looking at him, to be on the safe side. "I'm just working out how to get to the door."

"Ah!" said Eternal, knowingly. "You might want to think of a universal rule and break it."

Bea wasn't thinking about that: "Was my dad here?"

"Some American GI soldiers were shipped here to recuperate after the war in Vietnam," Eternal answered, pleased at the question. Bea peeped out of the corner of her eye to locate the voice. Eternal's face had replaced the GIs in the wallpaper. He had his sunglasses on.

"But unless your father was an old man when he conceived you, he wouldn't have been in Vietnam." The paper Vietnam soldier had stopped crouching and had stood up. "Would you like to explore the Vietnam war memorabilia in the corner?" asked Eternal, helpfully locating it with his gun.

Bea was disappointed; she missed a connection with a father she'd never really known and didn't understand why. "No, I wanted to see behind the door," replied Bea unenthusiastically.

"Try a universal rule," Eternal appealed.

Bea looked at the door, but her head felt full of her dad. *What would he think of me now, if he knew me? He would love me? Wouldn't he? Does he know my body's in a coma? Why doesn't he get in touch? Maybe he would now? If he knew?*

Eternal sighed impatiently and leant on his gun. "Ever felt like you were being pulled towards something?"

Bea considered the depressing feeling that overwhelmed her. "Yes, I think it's my coma, or the warehouse or the mattresses."

Eternal breathed deeply, in the way greater beings do in the presence of lesser minds, and kicked the gun so it spun around in his hands. He tried another hint: "If there was a force that held you to the planet, and you put on an astronaut's suit and floated into space ..."

"Gravity!" she squealed.

"Gravity will do!" shouted Eternal, as if he had scored a winning goal. "The law of attraction in relation to gravity! When you've broken this rule, there's eight to complete," he said in a disappearing voice.

Bea lifted off the ground. *Is attraction a rule? I don't think so, but gravity is. It's a planet rule, so it must be a universal rule.*

As she floated upwards, she felt the depressive hopelessness lift and found herself energised. "Wow! I am on battery recharge," she said. She glided round the warehouse walls, like a high-speed balloon, straight past the door. So, decided to fly a few circuits just for the sheer joy of it. *This is living!* She looked down at the forlorn, lost mattresses: old, grey, stripy, stained. Some torn, some almost new. *This is where the dead people's mattresses go. This is where my mattress will go, when I'm dead.*

The thought was deflating her. She was sinking towards the floor. "Oh no! Think happy, quick!" she cried to herself. Bea pictured her favourite happy thought: she had gone to an empty beach, one early morning with her mum on holiday. She lay down in the warm, dry sand and listened to the sea coming in. The sky was big and blue and endless and there was so much space that her head rested as if there was nothing but puffed-up clouds and big sky. She had felt peace. Then her gran rang, Mum started talking and it was gone.

Bea's head was banging on the warehouse ceiling, which was filthy. "Urgh." The thought of cobwebs was sending her downwards. She tried to think of a happy memory, but there was dust all over her PJ top and she couldn't think past it. She bounced off a mattress and fell forward onto her hands two metres from the door. Bea checked her PJ top several times for dust and shook her hair to be on the safe side. *I'm okay! There are no spiders. Dust doesn't kill! It doesn't!* She reassured herself with a few more hand sweeps. *I flew! Well, floated fast! Wow!*

Bea reached for the door. It unlocked, and Eternal stood in the door frame. He was wearing a GI uniform and a little GI hat had replaced his bowler. Even the swirling shapes in his shiny no-eyes were khaki. Bea felt a little irritated to see him so soon, and he sensed it.

"There are two ways to learn," said Eternal, with the resignation of one who knows the outcome already. "One can listen to the wisdom of the past or you can learn by experience. I suggest trying the first; the last is painful."

Bea was not interested in his lesson. He was blocking the door. *This door's magnetic, I've just got to get behind it! Magnetism. That's a universal rule for the future; I need to remember that word.* Bea noted her forward planning and was impressed. *I am clever really! He's right!*

Eternal did not move from the door opening. He was holding a large square box with a screen at the front and a wire thing sitting on top. It seemed awkward to carry and heavy. She'd seen the box in pictures at school – it was supposed to be a television, but she couldn't believe it had ever worked!

"Is this the health and safety talk?" she asked him. "Stay in twos and hold hands with someone else's sticky fingers."

"In an odd way, yes," said Eternal.

Bea was familiar with these before a field trip. She sat on the floor cross-legged, folded her arms and focused on the screen. Eternal looked mildly surprised at Bea's learnt behaviour. "This could be very informative if you listen carefully," he added kindly.

The screen flashed an ugly yellow light across its surface as it beamed into the greyness. On the screen, an old-fashioned man entered his living room and removed a cloth revealing a large machine. The film was in black and white. *How could people have watched this?* Bea thought, *without even the colour?* The old man cranked the machine, pulling levers and pressing knobs. A dial showing years reversed in time – the old man was travelling backwards through centuries. A pop-up label appeared in front of the film: H.G. Wells.

*Time, that's a universal rule. Everything exists in time. He's right, there's answers in this.* With increased interest, Bea focused on the screen, hoping to collect more universal rules.

Hitler appeared; everyone was saluting him with a hand gesture that would've been more productive on a basketball court. Another man she didn't recognise arrived. The name "Stalin" flashed automatically onto the screen. Troops were saluting him with a distant high five. *Why do groups of people have to have hand salutes? Is that so you can recognise the enemy? If so, wouldn't it have been better to do a complicated hand gesture? Complicated hand gesture*, she mused on her words. *My brain is trying new words and ideas all the while. What were my universal rules? Magnetism, see, where did that word come from?* Bea missed some of the screen images. It was hard to concentrate through the greyness.

President Truman arrived, his name helpfully written across the bottom of the screen, highlighted by images of a nuclear bomb; it was like a grey mushroom, no sparkles or lights. He sounded very important to himself: "With this bomb we have now added a new and revolutionary increase in destruction ... These bombs are now in production and even more powerful forms are in development. It is an atomic bomb! It is a harnessing of the basic power of the universe."

*Is this the health and safety bit? Atomic bombs? Atoms? Are they a universal rule?* Bea's thoughts flickered away from the screen.

Truman warbled on: "We are now preparing to destroy more rapidly and completely ... We have spent two billion dollars on the greatest scientific gamble in history ... and won ... both science and industry worked together under the direction of the United States Army."

Bea's thoughts took centre stage. *Why was he celebrating the potential destruction of the human race? The planet? The universe? As if it were a winning lottery ticket? Why would he be so pleased with himself?*

President Truman appeared in a different tie. "We must not continue to sacrifice the flower of our youth merely to check madmen, those who in every age plan world domination."

"You're a fine one to talk," Bea said out loud. "You're planning world destruction!"

Eternal tilted his head, interested in what she was taking in.

*This is like a bad old horror movie*, Bea thought. *Or something from the past that your teacher gets very excited about, and you can't understand why. So, the teacher talks about it even more, swinging their arms around and gushing words. In the end you just replay your favourite game sequence in your head and nod every now and then, hoping she'll stop.*

The TV didn't have good sound. It crackled out of a little speaker somewhere in the box. Bea missed something about pigs in a bay, and Cuba and maybe a whole chunk of other stuff. Her eyes wandered to the door opening behind Eternal. Two men in GI uniforms were crouched down in a ditch talking to each other. Then she recognised a name on the screen.

President J.F. Kennedy: "A man may die, nations may rise and fall, but an idea lives on."

*Maybe an idea is a universal rule. Everyone has ideas. I have ideas? Don't I? Or are they just other people's ideas living on? But ideas aren't alive. How do you know your idea is a new idea? No, I don't think it's a universal rule.*

Walter Cronkite appeared behind a desk labelled 'Walter Cronkite': "From Dallas, Texas, the flash, apparently official, President Kennedy died at 1 p.m. Central Standard Time."

*Death! that's a universal rule*, thought Bea. *Everything dies.*

'President Lyndon Johnson', (the president after Kennedy) a caption read at the bottom. *He put that in for me*, Bea thought. *He's realised I'm not that clever. But I'm getting universal rules out of this, so I can't be that stupid either!*

Johnson droned on: "The central lesson of our time is that the appetite for aggression is never satisfied. To withdraw from one battlefield means to prepare for the next."

*Too right, war, that's another universal rule. If it lives, it's at war with you, like the wasp! I've got loads of rules; what were they? Magnetism, death, time, not ideas, war.*

"The great society ..." Lyndon Johnson warbled on. "We will raise the monthly draft call from 17,000 to 35,000 a month ...". 'That's Vietnam soldiers' the caption read.

*This is all captions; I might as well read it.*

Then hippies were marching with banners saying 'love not war'. She recognised a banner, 'End Vietnam!'

Bea refocused. *This is about Vietnam. At last! Something relevant.*

Johnson continued: "In the words of the Bible, Hitherto shall you come, but no further."

"Good, is that the end?" asked Bea. She was getting tired of these world leaders and their black and white world.

"It's hardly started," said Eternal. He banged with a little irritated fist on the top of the TV and the film disappeared, "But these might be helpful" A series of symbols flickered onto the screen.

"I can't tell what colour they are, they're all black, white, or grey," Bea exclaimed. "A white triangle, three grey stars, a white triangle in a grey ball, a white cake with a piece cut out of it on a grey background, a butterfly? Possibly, if I squint? Is it a sight test?"

Eternal sighed a long, deep sigh; Bea had heard them a lot during her short life from various adults. The sigh said patience was a swimming pool and there was only a glass of water left. The TV turned itself off with a blink of old, yellow light.

"That was a nightmare!" she exclaimed, jumping to her feet and heading for the door. "How could they let their kids watch such bad graphics without colours!"

"Well, there's always the cold light of day to learn by," Eternal said, as if addressing someone else.

"Bea, did you understand the context of what is behind this door?" Eternal asked expectantly, letting the old TV box glide slowly to the floor in front of him.

"War is bad?" said Bea. "And you didn't need to hold that old TV but held it anyway. Why's that?" She leant against the door frame, craning her neck round to watch the soldiers. The scene was like colour TV had finally arrived, complete with lifelike animation.

Eternal sighed heavily and held his ground in the doorway. "Did you grasp any of the message within the film?"

Behind him, one soldier had a really large mobile phone connected to a huge battery on his back with a large stick coming out of it. The other one was talking to him and stroking his fingers along his gun as it rested on the edge of the ditch.

"You didn't answer my question," Bea said, aware Eternal was avoiding it.

"Really? Is that the best you can do?" He took his sunglasses off and popped them into the top pocket of his uniform.

Bea had heard this type of talk before and didn't like being asked to perform. "I think time is a universal rule," she said.

"No, it isn't," answered Eternal.

One of the GIs was holding up a postcard to the other one. They had a few sandbags around them. They appeared to be in a makeshift shelter in a field on the edge of a wood.

"Time is a universal rule," said Bea, keeping her eyes on the GIs. "Everything exists in it. You can't go backwards unless you break it."

"You cannot repeat yourself and make it a universal rule!" Eternal was exasperated.

He sounded like a teacher two minutes before lunch break, and she had had too much information washing through her head. It felt overloaded, and she was brewing agitation.

"What about war? That has a habit of repeating itself!"

"There's hope for you yet, Bea. Second rule: patterns repeat, the rule of correspondence." He tilted his head patronisingly. "You can break each rule once only. Are you listening?"

She spat the words into his face, "Break each rule only once," and pushed him sideways. He looked at her in amazement as he misbalanced and fell over the TV before righting himself with a sway of his body and slowly replacing his floating feet onto the floor. Eternal was not used to being shoved aside, and Bea had pushed past his limitless patience.

Bea walked through the door. Eternal turned towards her, wiping his face. "Experience is a harsh but thorough teacher if," he stressed, "you're willing to learn. Second rule: patterns repeat. Seven to complete." He grimaced and put his sunglasses on.

She gave him a Stalin salute and the door closed.

# 3

# Vietnam

The explosion pounded into Bea's ears, as a weight flung itself on top of her chest and threw her across the dirt onto her back. A wet mass of red particles rained into her face as she slid to a halt, bashing her hip against a ripped-apart tree trunk. Her ears were thickly thudding as she lay on the ground waiting for the next sensation. When it didn't happen, she opened her eyes to consider a blue and orange sky. When no one came to help her, she lifted her banging head to study the dead weight pinning her down. It was a GI torso. Well, a large portion of it was on top of her – some bits were missing, and there wasn't an arm on that side. She didn't search for the person's head in case it wasn't there.

"Are you okay? Could you get off me?" There was no reply.

*This is Eternal*, she thought, reorientating herself to the present situation. *He timed that on purpose. He knew I'd go through the door.*

She twisted her neck to look backwards at the door. It had disappeared. *I'll need to break another rule to get home, when I can think straight. Course he's disappeared.* Bea tried to push what was left of the GI off her chest. *What were the other rules? I can't remember. I used gravity and repetition, which is a shame – gravity would be handy right now.* She heaved at the GI's body again. *He's a dead weight. Get off me!* Bea was not surprised at the calm removal of her mind from an obviously traumatic situation. Everything was potentially traumatic to Bea. If she lost a sock, the trauma could send her over the edge of any reason she might have. So, it was best to tip over into 'calm removal' in truly dangerous situations. It was hard to think with the smell. *This GI hasn't washed in a while. That, or there's no deodorant in Vietnam.*

Reality slapped her face again. *I'm in the Vietnam war! I'm gonna die! No, I'm not, my body's in bed. It's just like a dream. A nightmare. Except I'm awake. Oh no! Why did I go through the door? This is why Eternal showed me the TV. Why am I so stubborn! Why do I have to learn everything the hard way! This is why there's computer games! So you can learn all the dangerous things remotely! Argh! Being me is so frustrating! Why can't I be somebody less incredibly stupid?*

She wiggled and twisted her torso trying to gain enough momentum to heave the GI's body off hers. She could smell his blood, and there was a wet patch seeping through her hospital gown except, looking at her sleeves, she wasn't in a hospital gown: she was in a GI uniform. *I'm a GI! I've gone through to the Vietnam war; I've gone back in time. Oh no, I'm stuck in the past! Like the man and the dial in the film footage! I'm not watching this – I'm in it. I've got to get out! I've got to get out!*

Bea was hyperventilating, with limited lung capacity, and was rapidly moving towards a blackout. "Jack! Jack!" said the GI standing over her. Bea refocused and her breathing slowed. "You took your time, get it off me!" she exclaimed. The GI scowled at Bea and rolled what was left of Jack off her.

He knelt down to examine him. "Jack! No man!" the soldier whimpered. He paused, choked by emotion, before he reached inside Jack's pocket to take out the wallet and pictures, finally pulling the dog tag off Jack's neck and placing it all in his inside pocket. He patted the torso affectionately. "I'll keep an eye on your son for you, buddy."

The GI ignored Bea, who was sitting up and looking at her jacket. "Ooh, I'm covered in blood," she said, examining the jacket. "Have you got a baby wipe? Or tissue? Look at the state of my jacket!"

The GI grabbed her by the shirt and lifted her up saying, "That was my friend ... Are you a woman?" he asked. "A nurse?"

He dropped her onto the floor again. "Sorry ma'am, my lucky day," he said eying her up as if she was a feast. He knelt on the floor next to her and leant in. "I'm Private Tanner," he said, smiling an unpleasant kind of smile.

Bea knew she was in trouble. He was zooming in for a kiss. *He has my surname. If this isn't my dad, maybe it's my grandad.* "I'm

Tanner too; we're related." Thinking quickly, she added, "I'm a boy!"

Eternal's voice crackled from the radio, stranded between herself and the deceased Jack: "Gender: universal rule number three. Six to complete," it sizzled. Bea wanted to talk to Eternal, not least because she'd changed her mind about being in Vietnam, and she wasn't totally convinced about the third rule. But Private Tanner was still leaning in on her.

"You're a guy!" he stated, as he looked her up and down and suddenly jumped to his feet. "Hard to tell with you new guys; you look like chicks," he said, somewhat confused and embarrassed.

Bea took the opportunity to scramble to her feet and examine her tall, male body.

"Wow, yeah, I'm a man," she exclaimed.

"I wouldn't go that far," said Tanner.

Tanner was lean, with a hungry edge, browned by the sun through a long stint in Vietnam. In his late twenties, he had the type of moustache she'd seen on The Beatles.

*Wow, I'm meeting my grandad for the first time! How bizarre! And he doesn't even know I'm his granddaughter!*

"I'm Bea," she said. Tanner turned away, she wasn't sure why, but she didn't bond easily with others, so it felt normal.

"I'm ... I've just arrived and got blown up!" *Don't call him grandad, call him Tanner. That's what men call each other: their surname.* Bea tried to separate herself from the blood-soaked jacket she was wearing, peeling it off with the sweat dripping off her. "It's a bit hot and sticky, isn't it? You haven't got a tissue, have you? No?"

"Better keep that on," Private Tanner spoke through gritted teeth, spitting out his words, without eye contact. "Grab Jack's banana radio. We better move out."

Bea examined her young man's torso underneath her khaki T-shirt. *Well, it's not the fittest, a bit chubby, could've been a better one. But it's male. I wonder what it looks like under its underpants? Better not look now.*

Bea picked up the large mobile phone and found it was attached to the battery pack with the large stick coming out of it. "Why do they call it a banana radio?" Tanner ignored her. She tried to push the stick down, but it didn't fold away. It just stuck up. She went to lift the pack and, even with her new muscles, the banana radio weighed a ton.

Tanner was watching, unimpressed. "Put it on," he said dismissively.

Bea tried to haul the battery onto her back, only to find she already had a backpack on and the radio wouldn't sit on top of the existing one. So, she put it on her chest. The stick got in the way but Tanner was already heading off without her, so it had to do. As she left, she wobbled towards the ground to pick up Jack's weapon. The weight of the banana radio caused her to misbalance and 'boof' went the gun-type thing into a set of trees, setting them on fire.

Tanner swung round and shouted: "What the hell are you doing? You crazy, stupid, infantile baby! Get your arse blown up! But don't jeopardise mine! Now get over here!"

Bea slowly raised herself onto her feet, looking at Jack. *He's going to be left here, dead. This isn't a game. He doesn't come back and get another go. It could be me, lying next to Jack. I could've died. Is it possible to be dead here and alive in the hospital? What would that mean? Would I just stay in a coma, or wake up?* She panicked, aware she could be on her own and turned to see Tanner stepping into the forest. She found it impossible to run with the weight on her, so she stumbled after her grandad, shouting, "Wait, it weighs a ton. More!" Tanner was waiting.

"Just 'cause you've got the same name doesn't mean we're related," he barked and looked at her as if he'd been dumped with a stray dog that was missing a leg or two. "You get me injured with your trigger-happy ways and big mouth and I'll shoot your head off."

*He doesn't mean that, because he'd be injured, so he'd struggle to hurt me, and I'd have to help him out of the forest, so he'd want me alive.* Bea was satisfied with her logical thought. *Wow, my thoughts are lining themselves up neatly like cars in a traffic jam. That's amazing!*

Bea continued a less focused conversation with herself. *So, what is Grandad's first name? I dunno. Maybe I never knew. How come gender is a universal rule? Isn't that a bit of a weak one? What if I say the wrong thing and use all the rules up and get stuck in Vietnam, like a toy action man?*

The radio antenna snagged on a tree. She tried to bend down, but she was taking the tree with her. She twisted and turned and the antenna got more tangled. She started to get angry, reached up, grabbed the tree and snapped off the offending branch. *That was easy. Hey this body's stronger than me.*

"Watch it," shouted Tanner. "Break that antenna and I'll break you! That's our ticket out of here, so look after it. Move! We're not going on a picnic in Mount Titicaca, you know!"

"Can you carry this? It's heavy."

"Shut up, new guy."

*Men are so rude to each other! And they don't help. Now I've got to carry this, or he'll think I'm a girl!* Tanner walked on, oblivious. She looked at her chubby arms with their underlying muscle. *I'm strong, but not strong enough to thump my grandad and live; he's too much like me.* Her strides were longer, if clumsy. I *want to stop for a wee, and a drink, but he's walking too fast and I'm not getting lost in a Vietnamese forest by myself. Do you think there's chocolate in the bag? Guess it might melt.*

They were following a worn route Tanner had obviously done numerous times, but he was still checking the ground carefully. She heard a distant machine gun to the right of her and threw herself on the ground. Tanner walked on regardless, so she got up. The trees were closer together and she had to watch for the antenna catching the trees, which made her neck ache. Tanner had stopped and was examining the ground carefully. Sweat trickled off his back from the humidity. Bea felt like a dripping sponge.

"Is it much further?" Bea whinged.

"Shut up. No one's talking to you," he replied as he concentrated on the path.

"Aren't we supposed to be on the same side?" she snapped back.

He turned, walked straight to her and pushed his face into hers: "Let's get this straight: you're new, you're a liability, you'll get me killed. I don't want you around me, so shut up and tuck in and we both might live."

Survival mode kicked in: "Ray!" she had remembered. "You're Raymond Tanner."

He was taken aback. Bea knew she had the advantage, she just had to tie Ray into looking after her somehow, so she'd live through Vietnam. *Okay, this is just like pizza on Friday night. I always get my way!*

"We're related" she exclaimed. Bea remembered Gran Tann visiting when she was little. Her mum and Granny Tanner did FaceTime ever since, but she'd never met her Grandad. Gran Tann was a skinny, hippy type, always going on about herbal remedies and healthy eating. Bea's weight was often mentioned, so Bea didn't have much to do with her.

"Who are you? You're not Matty's kid, are you?"

*Well, I have to be someone, and this is my grandad, after all.* "Yes," she lied, "they call me Bea, a nickname." *That was unconvincing.*

"Wow, you were a nipper when I last saw you. You can't be 16, surely? You don't sound like you're from the big apple?"

"They sent me to England," she quickly lied.

"We've gotta shift," said Tanner, and he began the uphill climb. "Wow, Matty's kid! Fancy drafting you in from England?"

*Don't say too much, and he'll just assume it all.*

"We're heading for the top of that next ridge." He pointed it out.

*That's too far to carry this stuff!*

"Miss the chopper and we're not getting another ride until tomorrow."

*Where's the taxis?*

"Put your feet in my footprints. That was a landmine Jack triggered."

*I'm in, he's hooked. Stuffed cheesy crust.*

"Stick with me, okay? Family, right?"

*Ham and pineapple!*

"Fancy that, huh! You look like our side, though!"

*With extra cheese.*

"How's your ma?"

"She cries a lot," said Bea honestly.

Tanner nodded, "That's your ma."

*And ice cream.*

"She must have wailed when you got drafted? You did get drafted, didn't you?"

Bea looked confused.

"You volunteered?" Tanner asked.

"Kind of," said Bea.

"Dumb-ass! You should be in school, growing your hair long and protesting against this war! What the hell are you doing volunteering?"

"I didn't know what it'd be like," Bea admitted honestly. *Woops! No ice cream!*

Tanner wiped his face with his hand and marched upwards through denser shrubs. "We could all be sent home next year if the peace protests keep up? Did you see it on the TV? Millions are marching."

"Yes," Bea said truthfully.

"And you still came! Bonzo! You might never have got drafted! Specially from England!" Tanner shook his head.

*Why did Eternal let me through the door? That's not very responsible for an adult. He shouldn't call himself a teacher! Teacher's come with you on field trips!* A foreign allegation fought back: *You chose to come through the door, rather than watch it all from a pathetic black and white screen. Eternal tried to stop you. Vietnam is not a field trip – it's a war!*

"What've you got there?" Tanner sighed. "You picked up Jack's Blooper? Did you pick up the grenades to go with it? What the hell are you doing? Where's your jacket? I told you to put it on! You're as white as a sheet of paper! Mud your arms and your face; you're a walking beacon. You dumb, stupid ...!"

Bea swung her fist round. The extra weight of the radio gave her additional momentum. It caught Tanner under the left side of his jaw and he reeled into a tree.

"Don't call me dumb!" Bea smarted.

Tanner pushed himself upright, "Well at least you got some fight in you, kid." He rubbed his jaw, and smiled. "Even if you are a bit stupid; save it for Charlie!" He indicated to the hidden enemy Bea had completely forgotten about. Tanner grabbed a handful of mud. "Cover your arms."

Bea felt better; she wasn't alone. Tanner would look after her. She scooped the mud out of Tanner's hands and shuddered as she dragged it over her arms. *Urgh, it's warm and sticky and there's insects wriggling in it!*

Tanner sighed, "You big girl!" He demonstrated for her to blot out her face.

Bea took a deep breath and applied the mud mask, it quickly hardened on her soft skin.

"See!" Tanner said. "You've got an M-79 grenade launcher and no grenades, get it?" He snatched it off her and offered her Jack's rifle. "Don't fire it! Not unless it's at my other leg." He hoisted his machine gun over his shoulder.

"Right Junior, let's get to the ridge and get the chopper outta here. We'll radio if we get there first. The rest of the unit are on their way."

Bea climbed out of the forest into a sparse, rocky patch of land, she could see some of the landscape, with a mixture of burnt forest, green forest, and fields in the valley below. The radio was sliding up and down her chest and catching on her belt, blistering her belly fat, as the radio grinded towards her belt. *It's impossible to carry this stupid banana radio comfortably, this is why they invented the mobile phone. Not soon enough. I could dump the radio, but Tanner would leave me, and the enemy would shoot me. And my belly hurts and I want to cry, but Tanner will know I'm a girl.* For the first time Bea could ever remember, she had to suck it up and be brave. She distracted herself with the M16 rifle. *It's solid, feels good, smooth. I wonder if many soldiers have carried it? And died? Maybe it's killed lots of people? Maybe it never killed one, and it just got taken off dead GIs.* Being a soldier wasn't what Bea had imagined. *Last resort, think of chocolate fudge cake, with a creamy chocolate topping.* It wasn't cheering her up.

As they entered into dense woodland, Bea listened to the unusual sounds of life still trying to exist in the war-torn land as she tried to concentrate on puzzling out the bigger picture. *Grandad is not a coincidence. Eternal knew I'd meet my grandad. Maybe Eternal wanted Tanner to look after me, even though he isn't doing a good job.* She shifted the rubbing radio up her body. *Maybe Grandad will tell me about my destiny? Or tell me something about my dad that explains my purpose? I wonder how old Dad would be?*

"Do you have a kid?" Bea asked.

"I dunno," Tanner stopped and sighed. "I dunno if it's mine. I got a card from my wife – she's just had our first, but the dates don't tally with my leave. I dunno if it's my son. Can you believe that?"

Bea thought of Gran Tann. *That's quite likely.* "Yes," said Bea honestly.

Tanner gaped at her: "Are you saying my wife would be unfaithful?"

Bea desperately wanted to drop the radio. She leant a hand against a tree to steady herself. "Well, you just wanted to … maul me!"

Tanner yelled in a whisper, "I'm in guddam Vietnam! Don't you ever, ever, mention that again!" Bea observed Tanner's face, reddened. His eyebrows dived towards his nose, "You'd think it's enough that we've come to this godforsaken hole to die!" Mean wrinkles deepened around his nose, as if they were permanently etched into his darkening face. "I don't give a crap if you lie in this mud and rot and neither does anybody else here!" The downturned mouth gaped like a mad fish. "Do you know how many Jacks I've seen?" His distorted face was the ugliest anger she'd ever witnessed. "Do you? You've no idea! You've no chance of making it through the first ten weeks! None at all! Huh?"

Bea wasn't used to people being more aggressive than her. She backed away from the red fury hurtling towards her.

"I've gotta lose a leg or arm to go home! Do you wanna choose that? Eh? Leg? Arm? Half my face, eh? I've two bullet holes. Look! Look!" Tanner showed a big scar on his shoulder and a hole in the side of his calf muscle. "They stitch you up and send you back out to get another one! I'm gonna die here! Like you! In Vietcong dirt, like Jack! Why?" He screamed up to the sky. "Why? I don't know!" He rounded on her, "You, tell me?" He gripped her by the shirt. "You're still in diapers! What the hell are you doing here? You know nothing!"

She was wincing, preparing for the thump. She didn't know where to look, but she didn't want to look into his face.

"What am I doing here? For the goddam USA that doesn't give a monkey's fart? For a whore of a wife?" Tanner was screaming at her.

*I've never been hit in the face before. It's going to hurt.* She wanted to scream, but nothing was coming out of her mouth.

"For who? For what?" ranted Tanner. He breathed and pushed her back onto her butt. "You're not worth it." He turned away and wiped his face, but his expression wouldn't come off; he'd tipped over into the redness of raw grief.

Bea was the only one there and someone had to feel his pain. He rounded on her again, "Three months, five days left on my draft. This is not our war! It's Charlie's war, nothing to do with us!

Charlie's taking the cities; we're not gonna win! I'm gonna die for what?" He grabbed her by the shoulder and pulled her up and spat the words into her face. "So some long-haired, hippy student can come back from his anti-war demo to my kiss my wife and kid, some slick, long-haired creep who's never lifted more than a banner in his life! I wasn't asking for much! A bit of loyalty!"

"Ray!" Bea whispered. He had tears in his eyes. "I don't know much about babies or women ...," Bea said desperately.

Tanner looked at her and let her go. "Course you don't. You're just a kid." He paused. "So, you've never had a woman?"

"No," said Bea, grateful to see him reconnecting.

Tanner looked at her: "Well, you'll get one here."

*Well, that's highly unlikely,* Bea thought.

"Thought of shooting myself," he laughed, as if it wasn't a joke. "Third strike and I can go home."

Bea was beginning to feel nauseous from the stress and the heat. Her senses heightened, she heard the sound of rustling behind her, cocked the M16 and aimed it vaguely in the direction of the bushes.

She felt the clout on the back of the head before she heard Tanner's whisper: "Numbnuts! It's a monkey! You idiot! Don't shoot it or Charlie'll come run you down, and you think you can leg it with that load you're carrying?"

The monkey's face blinked at her from behind a skinny tree, as if it agreed. Bea was too emotionally exhausted by Tanner's ranting to counter with a retaliation; she just wanted to breathe. She tried taking breaths, but they weren't coming. She was feeling woozy.

Tanner paused and rebalanced his emotions. His face softened. "Don't mind me, kid. I spent too long wanting to go home and all of a sudden, I don't know what it is any more." Tanner breathed deeply, "Let's get going," he groaned and walked upwards.

Bea, grateful for the end of the outburst, tried to inhale through the heat and the backpack and battery and the fear refusing to vacate her body. She'd got to climb the ridge. *Just keep moving,*

*Bea. You can do it, come on.* Her legs slowly obeyed. The trees were clearing and soon they were walking through ferns toward the ridge summit. She could see with relief the other GIs. As soon as Tanner saw them, he seemed to relax too, although his eyes were still scouting the ground.

*I've got to get back in Grandad's good books before we reach the others. Wow, I'm thinking ahead!*

Bea instigated a conversation, "What should I look out for on the ground?"

Tanner seemed pleased to share some of his warfare knowledge and described the landmines, punji spikes, traps and rigged explosives used by the Vietcong – whom he called "Charlie" – and the different tell-tale signs he was looking for. She knew he wouldn't normally make this kind of effort, but it was strengthening the family ties.

Bea was delighted to see three choppers in formation heading towards them. She dropped to the ground and threw the banana radio off. As it rolled onto the ground, she saw the large manufacturer's logo: a round, white symbol with a red outline and a piece of cake taken out of it. Obviously, it was supposed to be a radar because, underneath it in red letters, it said 'Radartrek.' She remembered the sign from the old TV. *But what have these signs got to do with anything? It's just nonsense.*

Tanner strode off, she guessed to grieve over Jack with some buddies. Bea examined her large blistering belly. *A good job it wasn't on my real stomach. Once we get to the camp I'll think up more universal rules to get me back in my lovely little body.* She breathed deeply as she looked out at the landscape below. It was a beautiful country, it looked so peaceful in places, but one side of the ridge was a swathe of burnt forest. Nothing was left but the tombstones of skinny tree trunks. They weren't charred – they were orange. In the distance, she saw a burnt-out village.

*They live with this war all the while; how do they do that? I just want to go home and be in my bed.*

Bea had never been in a fight with someone bigger. Tanner had frightened her. She'd felt the adrenaline, the uncertainty, the cold

33

sweat of recognition that pain was coming. *That's what it feels like when I kick off, and my mum knows, any time now, I might smack her one, and I do.* She felt a dread of understanding, like a shadow on her heart. *I have that angry face, that downturned mouth and fire in my eyes, that ugliness. Tanner's right: we are family.*

# 4

# A free-fire zone

Bea wasn't sure about the chopper; everything about it was unsafe: the blades, the lack of steps, its lack of wheels, the men inside it and the risk of the complete unknown. "Get in, soldier," the corporal shouted.

She hesitated, moving her hand over the white butterfly symbol on a square red background displayed on the helicopter door. *It's a propeller, with a small white triangle below it, a manufacturing sign. Why did Eternal show me company logos?*

The helicopter blades rotated and she felt the woosh of wind and dust. *Now or never; I can't be left behind.* She grabbed the handle and pulled herself into the cabin. Tanner was chatting to a GI with no shirt on his brown chest and postcards in his hat. He seemed to have been in Vietnam forever. He turned to inspect her. "Fresh meat," he said audibly.

The men sneered at her as if she was a dog turd. No one was going to give her a seat, so she tried to squash herself in by the window. No one moved.

"I need a seat," she said, not focusing on anyone.

Tanner looked embarrassed. She sat on a soldier's lap; he pushed her off and she fell on the floor. He and his mate laughed. She might have got up and thumped him but the helicopter swayed off the ground, so she clutched a seat leg with both hands and stayed on her bottom. The ground lurched away and her stomach followed.

"Shut the door!" she shouted.

"You shut it!" one of them jeered.

Bea clutched the chair leg tighter. *I'm not moving. I don't have a safety belt on or anything!* She stared out of the open door, horrified as the ground moved further away.

She saw devastation: areas of forest damaged as if locusts had eaten it, swathes of orange land filled with tree corpses. Between them were ordinary, sleepy forests and fields of normality. She wanted to go home, to be away from the soldiers' watchful eyes. Most of all, she wanted to be on the ground.

"Agent Orange," said Tanner, watching the horror on her face.

"America did that?" Bea asked.

Some of the guys jeered. One whispered loudly, "Commy."

"It's just strong weedkiller," Tanner explained. "Weeds grow back."

"Well, some do!" jeered the seat-hogger. "Some might not make it through the next mission. I give him two days."

"Ten dollars says one day," a GI piped up.

"That's my cousin's kid!" Tanner growled.

"I give him three hours then," said the experienced GI, laughing.

The helicopter was headed toward a dense patch of forest. In the centre a few shacks were surrounded by smoky clearings. To the north there was dense smoke and several planes were dropping bombs.

*It's just destruction*, thought Bea, searching for a universal rule but just coming up with gravity.

The pilot was checking with the corporal, and the chopper descended.

"Where are we going?" Bea asked. *Where's the nice little town or a clean military base with little rows of houses and some shops and a little apartment with a shower?*

"Down there!" said Tanner, looking as disappointed as she did.

*This is another mission!* she deduced. The unit seemed disheartened. *I guess they thought they were hitting basecamp too*, she groaned to herself.

Bea crouched down and watched the chopper leave in a cloud of dust. Tanner's face was etched with despair. She tried to avoid

Corporal Morales' determined group huddle because she didn't like close proximity and the men smelt of sweat. On the good side, someone else was carrying the banana radio.

Morales signalled for her to come and look at the map. *It's no good, I can't read the map, no idea where I am, but I bet I can read you, Morales.* Bea wasn't good at much and she knew it, but reading people was her special ability. *Okay, Morales, you're ultra focused on the job in hand, a career soldier, married to the army, you like control and you want something out of this mission: a medal? No, you've got several already.*

Morales looked up and caught her observing him. *This life has cost you – you're dead behind the eyes. Died a long time ago.*

Bea had seen that cold focus before, not always on the people she expected. People who had lost their passion and replaced it with an itch they couldn't scratch, mainly people in suits, like her headteacher. *Morales is addicted to war. That's a dangerous man.*

*My mind is super clear, like I can sense everything, but I'm not overwhelmed. The movement in the trees, the sweat dripping off Tanner, the level of heat, the tone of Morales. I'm becoming a superspeed highway, I can feel it! Wow, my chances of staying alive are much higher than all of yours.*

From what Bea could understand, their battalion had taken up position surrounding an enemy target. It was a large crater containing an entrance to a network of tunnels. The planes had bombed the area, but the choppers couldn't get in close enough, so they were going in by foot. Each unit had flamethrowers for the front to clear vegetation and possible enemy Vietcong. Blooper grenades were covering the sides, and 'Pig' machine guns would bring up the rear.

*Just look at all that information I've just retained. I don't normally remember things like that. My brain is amazing.*

"The good news is this isn't a stealth mission," Morales continued, staring at Bea, who avoided his eye. Morales did his serious operation expression, "This is a search-and-destroy mission, a recon by fire. Burn any village life, look for ammo, destroy food. Orders from the top: it's a free-fire zone. If they're in there, they are the enemy! Shoot non-combatants. Shoot on sight! Don't go into the tunnel; the tunnel rats will have laid mines. We'll blow the entrance up. We're flanked by units and, according to the radio, several are already in there, so let's get in there quick and help our guys out."

*Oooh Morales, you love this.* Bea thought. *I'll hang fire at the back and watch out for you.*

Morales thrust a flamethrower in her hand and smiled: "You're up front."

*Great! He's put me in front so I stand on a mine! Why waste an experienced man?* Her heart beat faster at the thought. She tried to breathe deeply to control her emotions, knowing they'd block her intellect.

"Do you know how to use this?" Tanner said quietly over her shoulder.

"No idea!" snapped Bea, hearing her supercool, tranquil sensation ebbing away.

He took a napalm cannister and loaded it into the flamethrower. "This is over 2,700 Celsius. Boiling water is 100 Celsius, get it! It's hot! the pain is incredible! Don't burn yourself, or us! Aim over there," he directed, "and squeeze the trigger slowly."

Bea held the flamethrower steady and squeezed a little too fast; it set the forest on fire, melted and died within seconds.

"Lesson over, move out," snapped Corporal Morales.

"Keep your eyes on the floor," Tanner hissed at her.

A sudden thrill of power at joining the destruction enthralled her. *If I'd had lessons like this at school, I'd have learnt a lot quicker! I'm a fire-starter!* All the energy she'd wanted to blast at this miserable company of men she could discharge into the forest. *I'm going to explode my way to the enemy camp!* She took a step forward and heard a twig break. She carefully took her foot off and remembered the mines. *I'll aim the flamethrower towards the floor 5 metres ahead, then I can catch the mines and booby traps before they detonate.* She squeezed the trigger and a ball of flame shot into the forest, and the tree in front of her evaporated.

"Over here, airhead," shouted Morales. "At least move in the right direction." The others jeered.

Bea breathed deep satisfaction. She had the ultimate destructive force in her bare hands and every instinctive atom said to flash-fire Vietnam to the ground. She moved over to the where her team were loading their weapons. She watched the cloud of smoke come up from a nearby unit already halfway down the descent and spotted a squirrel flying with little furry wings through the trees away from the smoke, followed by a monkey squealing in fear.

*It's not just trees.* A tense, dark dread shadowed her heart. *I'm going to kill every living thing in my path. Even if it's Vietcong, I'll be a murderer.* The fear expanded into her whole being. *Who am I really? Who might I become? Can I kill someone? Maybe today I'll become dead behind the eyes, like you, Morales.* She felt her eyes smarting. *It's just napalm smoke.* She knew the answer – she just had to admit it to herself.

Morales pushed her forward and she focused on the descent. She adjusted the squeeze on the flamethrower, letting out a short burst to form a path. Treading carefully, she searched for wires, raised ground and spikes. After 400 metres the cannister ran out. Throwing the old cannister to the ground, she recognised the red and white triangle logo. Underneath, it said Chemoxic Corp. *All the symbols must be company logos,* she assumed. The flamethrower was getting heavy on her arms but she reloaded, squeezed again and walked forward. *I've become a soldier.*

She heard a chicken clucking. *I'm gonna cook a chicken*, she thought, but the chicken never crossed her path.

Instead, a man did. She hardly saw him when she heard Ray shout, "Down", and she dived for the dirt. She heard Ray and Morales' machine gun fire flitting through the air above her and saw the zinging bullets hit the Vietcong before he dropped back in a heap of stillness. He lay in front of her. She was motionless, waiting for more Charlie to come out of the woods. They didn't. She stared at the clearing ahead and heard the screaming of men and women, guns firing, GIs shouting. She felt extraordinarily serene. She sensed everything. She instinctively felt the path was clear and was the first to stand. When she saw a GI step into the path, she registered him at lightning speed and let her weapon relax. She was gaining confidence.

Morales strode by her, pushing her out of the way, and led them into the smoking village. Anything that hadn't been bombed had now been set alight. Two soldiers were tipping over oil and rice to the left side of Bea. The GIs stepped back and signalled a free hand to her, so she torched it.

The ground shuddered as the tunnel entrance was blown to pieces. It caught her off guard and, again, she dived for the dirt. She looked up and the two GIs were sniggering at her.

Bea rolled over to face the bodies of a skinny Vietnamese couple and their 6-year-old child lying on the ground holding a dead cat. She jumped up. *They've killed everything, including the cat! A free-fire zone, kill non-combatants, means killing kids and cats.*

Further away were another two bodies: two men who weren't holding guns. *Are they civilians?*

The experienced GI from her unit walked nonchalantly by with an armful of Vietcong rifles and some grenades hanging out of his hands, heading into the forest. The GIs were beginning to relax; *the GIs are assuming if the Charlies aren't dead, they're trapped in the tunnels. Of course there'll be another entrance, deeper in the forest.* A few of her unit were assigned to watch the bush, including Bea.

She saw them dragging the dead family away to a large pile of bodies. She was grateful she wasn't being asked to torch them. The cat lay in the dirt. Tears rolled down her face. *I don't know who I'm crying for, the Vietcong family, the men who didn't want to be here, the cat. No, I'm crying for me. I don't want to be here, looking at this. I'm just a kid.* It was impossible to wipe away the flow of tears with her vest.

Tanner was a reassuring sight observing his own section of bush. *This is why Grandad is so angry; it's pointless butchery.* The units were radioing to disperse. A corporal shouted to Tanner that the tunnel entrance was secure, and they were heading off to meet the choppers at the original clearing. Tanner pulled some gum out of his pocket and chewed on it. *It's over, I can go home.*

Then Morales stepped out of the trees with two of the unit GIs and two prisoners – an old Vietcong shuffling unsteadily on his feet and, helping him walk, was a boy of about 10. Morales shot a look at Bea and noted her red eyes. Again, Bea felt the dread of the inevitable. Her senses were heightened by Morales' presence, the superspeed highway returned and she immediately calmed. This man had no limits and she instinctively knew it. At his presence, soldiers disappeared into the jungle and the five GIs were instantly alone with the prisoners. Bea checked for backup among the men. Their eyes were on the ground. *They know what's coming.*

"Killed anyone yet, son?" Morales drawled.

Bea observed him closely, surveying the situation.

"Do you know if you can?" Morales was assessing her. "If you can't do it now, when you're face to face with Charlie, he'll shoot you first. You need to know you can do it, understand?"

*I understand. This is some kind of initiation ceremony for new guys.*

Morales held out his rifle to her. Bea scrutinised the men, who were all watching her. "You need to know I can shoot someone, so you all feel safer," she said.

She snatched Morales' rifle off him. *Your rifle is safer in my hands.*

Tanner groaned, "Not the kid, Morales, just the old guy."

Morales examined Bea closely. "He'd shoot you. Can't be much in the age. Four years?"

The old guy, aware of the situation, began to beg for the child. "No sol-yer, no sol-yer, child." Bea registered the despair and heartache, tears formed in his eyes, but she felt cold, steeling herself for the situation.

"How many of our men do you think this old guy's shot, uh?" Morales pushed the old Charlie to his knees.

"No sol-yer," the man carried on, begging.

Tanner spoke up, "Not the kid. Look, I'll do the kid. Give junior the old guy."

"Deal," said Morales. "Show him how it's done, Tanny." Morales pushed the child to his knees and held him down with one hand, side-stepping to avoid the bullet's path. The boy gazed helplessly at the old chap, as if the world was too painful, but his grandfather was still safe.

The old man was searching each soldier for compassion, tears pouring over his face. "Child. Child," he wept.

Tanner raised his gun and hesitated.

"Child," the grandfather implored Tanner.

"Don't prolong the agony, Tanny," Morales drawled. Tanner took a slow, careful aim. Bea, with an inspired moment of recognition, realised, *He's not going to shoot the boy*. She moved her rifle slightly to the side and squeezed the trigger. The bullet escaped and shot Tanner in his other calf. His leg buckled and his rifle went off in the air.

The unit looked at her, shocked. Tanner was livid and Morales stunned. It took a millisecond for her brain to draw its conclusion. She raised her gun and, now with some confidence, efficiently squeezed the trigger in Morales' face. *Not a bad shot for close range*. His body swayed momentarily and he dropped back.

"Well, I've shot someone now!" Bea stated defiantly.

The two remaining GIs were backing off from her. *That's right. You might not have totally agreed with the situation or liked Morales for it, but I'm an unknown entity, and I might get rid of witnesses.*

"Child," the old guy was still weeping, as he registered the new situation. Bea signalled with her head to the boy to run for the trees, but he helped his grandfather to his feet. She aimed her rifle at the two GIs, to cover the old man hobbling for the forest. They dropped their guns and put their hands up.

Tanner was grabbing his calf muscle: "I'm family. What the hell?"

"Three bullet wounds and you get to go home, Ray," Bea smiled. "One to remember me by."

He looked at her with recognition, as if he'd really seen her, and then at Morales' body, then at the other GIs, who were still gawping at the immensity of the situation.

Tanner grabbed the end of her rifle and lowered it. "One step closer to home, guys," he winced to the other GIs. "Get going. I'll sort this." Reassured by Tanner, they collected their rifles and headed off into the forest.

Tanner motioned for her to pass him the flamethrower and, with one short blast, Morales melted into the Vietnamese earth in a charred mass. *He never took Morales' dog tag off, but I'm not going to search for it – he looks like just another Vietcong body.*

"Help me up," Tanner said, holding out his arm.

The gunshots rang loud and clear in the forest, and she heard the old man shout "Child, child," and the crash of the small body on the brittle, burnt-out trees.

# 5

# World order

The chopper was silent. Tanner had been medevacked to the hospital. The men's bravado dissipated with Morales' charcoaled corpse; they were busy with their own feelings. They glanced at Bea with suspicion and respect. *Apart from the experienced GI, they're all draftees. None of them would have signed up for this.*

She sat on a seat reflecting out of the window, still clutching Morales' rifle. She felt older. Life had changed and there was no way back. She was on her own, but she felt centred, as if she'd lost her fear of everything.

She reproduced the situation as if it was a screen in front of her, rewinding to the episodes she wanted to revisit, astonished at her detailed picture of events. *The Vietnamese kid died anyway; I didn't change anything. I killed Morales. I should feel bad about that; I'm not sure I feel anything. I don't even know if it's real; it's the Vietnam war – my body's comatose in the twenty-first century. Grandad gets to go home and spend his life listening to Granny Tanner go on about how he shouldn't eat chocolate. Tanner's baby might be my dad, my dad might spend time with his dad, if he's his dad. Won't change anything for me. So, why am I here?*

*Why did I kill Morales? I dunno, it was just instinctive. I felt superfast, alive, fully aware in those few seconds. Maybe this is my purpose? My destiny is to be a killer and Eternal knows it. Am I a killer? Morales is really dead now, even when I return to my body, he'll still be dead.*

The chopper landed at a base with a long airstrip. There weren't any real roads, just compressed dirt. Two concrete buildings formed dark shadows against a setting sun – a small hospital and command centre. Apart from that, the troops quarters were in sandbag shelters.

As they disembarked, the darkening camp echoed with voices and the odd song. She strolled by a Quiet Hawk plane preparing for the nightshift of evening surveillance, and immediately spotted the manufacturing logo: three white stars.

Two base police arrived to escort her off the airfield. *News must travel at the speed of banana radio.* They delivered her to the command centre, marching her upstairs to a corridor of private dorms. She entered the one labelled "press". A whitewashed room, containing a bunk, table, chair, an ensuite sink and loo. *At least it's not sandbags and dirt. This room must be top-of-the-range Vietnam.* Her attendants left, but she heard their feet shuffling behind the door.

She seized the chance of a strip wash; she'd been sweating in the heat and still had mud on her arms and face. There was only one tap, cold, but in Vietnam that's all you needed. There was a bar of soap and a rough, worn towel. *Guess this is luxury!* She got the chance to examine her male body and her new manhood. *It's not such a big deal, but the stubble on my chin is really annoying. How do they live with that?* They brought her food and a mug of coffee and, at last, she lay on the bunk to think.

*This is pretty good treatment for a criminal. There's no TV. It's probably just an old grey box like Eternal's. Where is he, anyway?* Her brain was settling back into a settled state now she'd relaxed. *I know I'm in trouble, but what can I do? I just need some universal rules to get home.* All Bea could focus on was death, the Vietcong family lying on the ground, Morales and the fact she was now a killer.

The door opened. She'd expected Eternal, but she got Sargent Major Milton. "To your feet, private," he announced. Bea had forgotten she was still in the army, so she got to her feet and tried her best at an American salute.

He was a middle-aged man, his wrinkled eyes turned down towards the outside of his face, as if sheltering his vision from a world he'd seen too much of. *He's been in the army too long, he's unfazed by this situation. He sees a mixed-up kid who has been asked to do more than any decent human being should do, which is true.*

He pulled his chair towards the bunk. "Sit down, private," he said, gesturing to the bunk. He took his hat off, brushed his trousers

45

down and laid it carefully on his lap. "Tell me about the incident with Morales and Tanner, in your own words."

Bea had already gone through the events in her head trying to work out what she should lie about. In the end she opted for the following version of events. She explained she'd been asked to shoot two civilians; one was a kid. The rifle had gone off in the stress of the moment, and she'd accidentally shot Tanner in the leg. Morales had asked her to execute the child. She thought that unreasonable and so, in the stress of the moment, she shot him and torched the body.

Milton nodded. "That's murder of a superior," he said, "a very serious offence."

*Well, technically yes.* Her palms were sweating.

Milton continued: "That's not what I heard happened to the honourable officer Morales. Private Tanner, your cousin, I believe, explained that your unit was in a combat situation against the Vietcong, on a special mission. Private Tanner was injured and Morales rescued him at great expense to himself. Morales was blown up rescuing Tanner and died from those injuries on the field and, as such, he is another United States hero. His widow and children and country can be very proud of the sacrifice he made. As a result of that sacrifice, his widow will get a full widow's pension to care for his children and he will be given another purple heart for her to treasure."

"Oh," said Bea, completely thrown by the scenario presented.

"I'm inclined to believe Private Tanner's version of events. Isn't that what really happened, Private Tanner?" Milton asked.

"Um, yes," said Bea.

"Private Tanner has suffered his third bullet wound, so he'll be going home a hero with a medical discharge." Milton continued, sighing: "Unfortunately, being shot by incompetent boys new to the field is as common as infected wounds, but we never mention either on discharge papers."

"Oh," said Bea. *He knew the truth before he'd even entered the room.*

Milton replied, "Good. That account of events is already circulating around the camp and, after a good night's sleep, you'll be returned to your unit in the morning. Try not to discharge your rifle near your own men for a few weeks. Sleep well, Private Tanner, enjoy the luxury." He gestured to the room and Bea realised he meant it. "Don't bother getting up." With that, Milton collected his hat and left.

Bea was stunned and lay back on the bed. *They want a cover-up! Not just for Morales' widow and children, but the press back home and the morale of the camp. Guess they don't want half of these troops thinking they'll end the war by shooting their officers.* She took a deep breath. *There is no justice in war. I just need to get out of Vietnam now.*

"I'm ready to break a universal rule!" Bea announced loudly to the empty room and waited three seconds before Eternal arrived through a wall, in a judge's gown. The wig was small, white and she wasn't sure how it was staying on his head. The swirling shapes in his eyes were hardly visible against the light behind them. She was pleased to see him but wasn't going to show it. She wanted to go home.

"Well, it appears you've been found guilty of murder," Eternal stated smugly.

"Hardly!" said Bea, not bothering with eye contact. *He knows everything, anyway.*

"But you did shoot someone and they died," Eternal declared, still with an edge of conceit.

She sighed. "I'm ready to go home. This is Vietnam! A real war. They shoot people and they gave me a gun! What did they expect?"

"And who is the enemy, Bea?" Eternal asked helpfully.

"Anyone that pisses me off!" said Bea, to herself and with a total acceptance of the truth.

"So, you are the judge?" asked Eternal, spinning his wig and finding it didn't sit any better when it returned to its original position.

*He's going to make this hard work. I'm going to have to engage with him to get home.* She sat up and stretched: "Everyone is judging all the time. They think it's a pointless war! Tanner doesn't believe in it. Most of the soldiers don't."

"Ah, you met your grandfather," Eternal said, as if he obviously knew that.

Bea stood to walk the stiffness off. "You knew I would. He's right: this whole war is pointless! It doesn't make any sense. Why would America be in Vietnam?"

"To reduce the population of the USA," Eternal said nonchalantly. "Fewer men, fewer families, more wealth to spread around. They're helping to get the US out of its economic slump ..."

Bea interrupted, "You're joking! It sounds like they're being sent here to die on purpose!"

"War is big business Bea," said her life teacher.

Bea stopped in her tracks. *That's why he'd shown her the manufacturing logos.* "They are making millions out of this."

"Billions," calculated Eternal.

"The choppers, the Quiet Hawk, the napalm cannisters, the radio."

Eternal interrupted: "The base you're in. The factory's built to make the kit you use, the parts to service them, the latest technology and weaponry. It's all helping the US become the great USA."

Bea interrupted: "This is all to make money?"

Eternal continued, "To create progress, and establish a greater destiny."

Bea visualised the black and white film. Information was slotting together in her head like a jigsaw. *It's a weird sensation – I've never found jigsaws easy – but the pieces of this puzzle want to pull together.* "Kennedy was against the war!" she announced, as if it was a headline revelation.

Eternal was pleased: "Kennedy was against progress, against world order."

"I thought Kennedy wanted peace."

Eternal sighed: "He wanted an end to the arms race."

Bea was getting frustrated: "It's the same thing! Isn't that peace? How can there be world order in an arms race?"

Eternal, self-righteously, picked up a metal pen out of his pocket and an empty screen appeared. He tapped it a few times in different places. He was obviously seeing something she wasn't. Then words appeared on the white wall:

Assignations between 1920 and 1979:

1920 – Supreme Ruler of Russia and President of Mexico

21 – Prime Minister of Spain and Portugal and Japan

22 – President of Poland

23 – Bulgaria

24 – Sudan

26 – Ukraine

28 – President of China

32 – France and Japan again,

33 – Peru, King of Afghanistan

34 – Prime minister of Romania, Austria and King of Yugoslavia

Then a break. Bea thought, *that's the Second World War.*

45 – Prime Minister of Egypt

46 – King of Siam and president of Bolivia

47 – Burma

48 – Yemen

49 – Syria, Iran and Sarawak and so it went on again affecting Malaysia, Pakistan, then Central America, Jordan, Ceylon, Ethiopia and African countries

1963 – Nov 2, Ngo Dinh Diem, the President of Vietnam

1963 – Nov 22, John F. Kennedy, the President of the United States

"They took them both out in the same month! It was all planned, all of the leaders, by who ...?" Bea asked, amazed.

"The world order," Eternal stated. He seemed pleased at the progress of his student.

"You mean a secret society of assassins?"

"A global financial movement" He corrected.

Bea pondered the list. "Why didn't they bother during the Second World War? It would have been the perfect time to get rid of a few heads of state?"

Eternal waited for the penny to drop.

"Because they were behind the war, behind Hitler and Stalin," Bea exclaimed.

She heard Winston Churchill's voice echo into the room. "We must go on. It must be world anarchy or world order. Throughout all this ordeal and struggle, which is characteristic of our age, you will find in the British Commonwealth and Empire good comrades to whom you are united by other ties besides those of state policy and public need."

Bea was confused. "And these other ties are money and destiny? But this is real people, real lives, thousands and thousands of real people! Grandad got shot three times."

Eternal interrupted, "And lived!"

Bea was getting annoyed. "Thousands didn't. They just died here! On this soil"

Eternal paused: "Do you want justice? Do you want to die for the crime you committed against Morales? Weren't you relieved Milton just let you off the hook?"

Bea paused: "What's that got to do with it?"

Eternal sighed, dusting his glasses and placing them on with a single hand. "We don't always get justice. Sometimes there are bigger things at stake. They work in our favour, or not. We get

50

progress, we get destiny. Your destiny was to get Milton; you could've got Yancy."

The door opened and Sergeant Major Yancy walked in. Eternal vanished.

"Really!" said Bea, whispering behind gritted teeth to the vanishing teacher. "Is this just some big life lesson to you! I need to go home!"

She knew straight away what Yancy was, because shuffling behind him, in handcuffs, wearing brown, cotton-stained shorts and T-shirt was the old Vietcong man from the search-and-destroy mission. Yancy was huge trouble.

He didn't speak. He was assessing Bea and, already, she wasn't adding up. The old Vietcong looked at his feet. Bea did a half-cocked American salute and tried to stand to attention. Yancy didn't ask her to sit down.

Bea's brain tipped quickly into the super-calm highway speed. This time the transition felt smooth and purposeful. Her senses adjusted and she began to filter out the knowledge she didn't need: the smell of the old man; the heat growing in the small room; the blistering burn from the banana radio; ticking of the alarm clock on the table; the officer who closed the door and stood behind it tapping his foot; the taste of spag bol still in her cheeks.

*That feels better. I wish I could always do that.*

Bea studied the incoming. *Yancy's a good fifteen years younger than Milton, so mid-career, hungry for a move up. Soft hands, without a tan, been at a desk job longer than he'd been in the field. He's cock-sure to the point of arrogant, keeps himself in trim, he must always be in the mirror, a bit of insecurity under the veneer. This man needs to prove to himself who he is.*

*Wow, what a brain when I use it!*

"I thought you might be a draft-burner? A peace protester? But you're not, are you?"

"No," said Bea truthfully. "Sir," she added, remembering she was a GI.

"You a Christian, Quaker, religious objector? No, I don't think so."

"No, sir," said Bea.

"You might be a commy? A traitor?"

"I dunno. Sir."

Bea completed Yancy's assessment: *He likes to be right. He doesn't want the answer – he wants to figure it out. He's too competitive. He likes the game and wants to win. He has to win. He's already set the game up, that's why the old man is here.*

"You don't like authority!"

"That's right, sir," said Bea honestly. *He needs to win. Let him win.*

"You're a wild card. A natural born killer. You just do as you feel."

*He's good, but I'm not a natural born killer, hopefully!*

"No, sir," she replied.

"Ah," said Yancy. "But you're not sure cause you're still young. You think there might be hope for you?"

He was toying with her and beginning to get on her nerves now. She shuffled and looked away.

"Easily agitated are we, soldier?" Yancy's assessment was complete. "So, you shot your officer, Morales, rather than follow an order, did you?"

"He asked me to shoot a kid."

"I thought he asked you to shoot this Charlie here," he motioned to the old man, "on a search-and-destroy mission with a command to kill on sight all non-combatants, a free-fire zone, no survivors expected. Did you do that, soldier?"

The old man was watching. *He might not understand everything we're saying but he's picking up the tone. He knows it's not good.* She looked him in the eye and he gazed back.

"No. Sir."

"Do you know him? Ever met him before?"

"Only the once."

"Does he remind you of anyone back home? A grandpappy?"

"No," said Bea. "Sir."

"Always the pause for the 'sir'," said Yancy.

"Brought up in England and we don't say that. Sir."

"Do you know how to follow orders in England?"

Bea sensed what was coming.

"Yes. Sir."

"Did Officer Morales ask you to do anything unreasonable when he asked you to kill a Charlie in a free-fire zone? To kill on sight?"

"He wasn't running. He'd been captured."

"Not the point," said Yancy. "It was a free-fire zone. Did you follow orders? No, you didn't."

The pistol came out of the back of his trouser belt. "Now, you're gonna shoot that Charlie and follow orders, aren't you, Private Tanner?"

"Nope. N.o. No! I am not!" said Bea, tipping beyond calm and into boiling point.

Yancy pointed the gun directly at Bea's head. It was a just out of arm's reach. He drew another pistol out of his pocket. *I'll have to shoot this officer too.*

"There's no option of shooting me, Private Tanner. Don't go there!" Yancy was one step ahead. Bea had to get control of her temper. "One of you is gonna walk out of here," Yancy pushed. "Which is it gonna be?"

The old man understood the situation. He was nodding at her and smiling as if to say, "Shoot me." "Child," he said. "Child," and he dropped to his knees.

*He can see I'm a child*, Bea studied the old man. *They'll kill him anyway, he knows it. He's seen what I've done, now he's offering his life. Why would you do that for me? The US enemy? It doesn't make sense.* He nodded again, giving his permission.

"Well, soldier?"

*This is just a game*, Bea thought. The calm restored itself. She took a deep breath. Yancy measured it. *Eternal's put him up to this, to prove his point.*

"Nope, you'll have to shoot me." She looked Yancy in the eye. *He isn't going to kill anyone; he's making his point.* She turned just like the 10-year-old boy had to fix her eyes on the wrinkled face and warm, open, almond eyes of an old grandfather of Vietnam. *He has more dignity than anyone I've ever met here. I like him.* Bea lost interest in Yancy; he wasn't important.

Yancy was not going to lose. "We do not tolerate dissention on the battlefield. Officers will not die by the likes of you."

She heard the trigger, and the bullet leave the gun. It caught her by surprise. She heard the cry of the old guy, and saw an expression of compassion hit his face. What she hadn't expected was the thump of a small stone hitting her neck, the sharp stab of her windpipe opening. "Death," she whispered as she lost consciousness and flopped backwards to the ground.

# 6

# The Presence

There should have been a pause, something to signify the huge moment of her death, but the truth was Bea was already scrutinising an intensely blue sky, and upside-down trees hanging from it. *Wow, they're upside down*, she thought, with insight.

She watched three giggling people float by holding hands, as they parachuted upwards to the inverted trees, without any parachutes. The next moment, she too had landed on the ground with a small thud, next to them, face down in lush, bright grass. She rolled over laughing, to face three equally ridiculous people in a balloon basket. A fourth person in colourful clothes and a floppy hat was scrambling into the basket in an undignified manner. When everyone's legs were inside, the basket wobbled and set off into the sky. There was no balloon attached.

Bea experienced sheer, joyful light-heartedness for the first time. There was nothing to rankle her completely blank brain, except the ribbon dancing and twisting as it hung from the wicker basket. So, with a small burst of light energy, she jumped up and gripped the ribbon with one hand, and floated effortlessly into the sky under the basket.

A young man's face peered over the edge, expressing daft delightedness to see her hanging from the ribbon. She heard him explaining they had a hitch-hiker to the other occupants in a language she couldn't understand. The rest of the crew peered over the edge and the basket tilted lopsided, until they were all in danger of falling out. They waved and cheered to Bea. *Hello,* she thought happily, waving back, and then they all rushed to the other side, chatting and laughing, in an attempt to rebalance the basket.

The basket caught a breeze and coasted upwards. Below her was a lush and picturesque country filled with vivid, almost edible colours. She drank in the space, the colours, the textures of trees and crispness of detail. She felt increasingly satisfied as meadows and forests, hills and valleys, skylines of blue and purple mountains nourished her with intense texture and tinted with sky reflections. Even the snow hanging within the clouds and dusting the mountains filled the depths of her aching. *This is better than any meal I ever tasted.*

The Kingdom was so real that it thrilled each sense. The scent of warm grass and forest trees carried on the breeze, as it touched her cheeks with such a gentle, warm caress that she felt held and comforted. She could hear leaves shivering with delight, the basket creaking, small birds thrilled at existence, a cockerel triumphant with the day. Each sound increased her pleasure. She tasted the willow of the basket, the blossom and pine in the breeze. She was satisfied by being.

The basket drifted downwards and Bea absorbed herself in investigating the individually designed homes each with its own garden. Some were together, some on their own. Each place was uniquely created and extraordinarily beautiful, as if every detail had been carefully thought through to please its occupant. There was a bamboo house on stilts, over a river, with a little watermill attached. *Oh, I love that one.* A small cottage with a mossy roof snuggled in the hill with a garden that fanned out in different directions, with such an incredible range of colourful plants. *Oh, I love that.* A stone house almost floating out onto a lake with stone steps to hop onto. *Oh, I love that.* So it went on, with each one beautifully crafted with tenderness and care and consideration in natural materials and an incredible arrangement of plants that proudly displayed their finest texture and colour.

*Oh! There's a hole in the ground!* Sky popped through it and a small cloud puffed its way up. Bea knew with certainty that below this landscape was another world of colour and layer. *So, there must be layers above this one too, this Kingdom is full of layers, as high as it is wide.* In some parts of the pastured landscape, there were lots of irregularly shaped holes. With each one Bea felt, in the absence of anything, an anticipation of what might be.

The wicker basket hovered over an absent space. The occupants whispered quietly among themselves. The sky within the hole retreated, and a new landscape formed. The occupants "oohed".

A small hillock bounced up through the mud and a large foundation stone rose out of the knoll. A spring waterfall squeezed past the rock and formed a new, sparkling stream. The basket occupants gasped in delight as trees and bushes of different sizes and shapes and colours came out of the ground, competing for attention to display their best shape, colour, blossom and fruit until each reached its intended size.

Hundreds of people came, like little ants, laughing and talking, towards the new landscape. Everyone was carrying something. Soon they were putting together a wooden house with a spiral staircase on the outside of one corner and a little tower on the other and a balcony between the two. *Oh, I love that one*, Bea thought. The external house was complete. Still more people came, bringing furniture, rugs, bedding and crockery. She felt the rocking of an armchair as it was placed on the balcony, heard its quiet, rhythmic creak, knowing it would soothe heartache and restore joy.

Flowers and smaller bushes popped up, arranging themselves around the gardens and children ran about sprinkling seeds so that, in the blink of a summer afternoon, a multi-coloured flower meadow shimmered in the sunshine.

Finally, everyone stood quietly for a moment and admired the new home. A ray of sunshine lit up the roof and Bea felt a warmth and love she'd never been aware of. Everyone waited for the occupant. Bea desperately wanted them home. She hungered for it, aching with the anticipation. She craved their arrival.

A small person walked up the hill. Bea couldn't see them clearly but she was bursting with the warm tenderness and incredible joy of a long-awaited friend. The occupants of the basket were jumping up and down and throwing confetti and rose petals out of the basket. Bea cheered and shouted, caught some falling petals and threw them into the sky. On the ground, people were jumping up and down and clapping, and she could see the person being hugged by each person they met.

*This person is incredibly popular; everybody loves them! They must be so special, and amazingly kind to be loved like that. No one would build a place like that for me.* The belief filled her with a heavy sadness; the basket above her faltered. The occupants gasped in surprise as the basket dropped a few metres, then plummeted. *Uh oh! Think happy thoughts.* The basket occupants yelled with fright as they passed Bea, still holding tightly to the ribbon, a hundred metres up in the air. *I can't think while I'm falling. Help!*

Beneath them, a white cloud opened in the sky and a giant of a man walked out of it. He was semi-translucent, as if made up of millions of raindrops. He strolled nonchalantly up some cloud steps that appeared just before his feet needed them and dissolved shortly after his feet left them. He caught the basket with one hand and gave a broad smile to the occupants before puzzling over Bea bouncing on the end of the ribbon. Bea did her best at a friendly smile. The giant picked Bea off the ribbon by her collar and, with one blow of his breath, the basket skipped back onto an air current. The occupants floated off cheering and waving to the giant and chatting to each other about their narrow escape. Bea was dangling from his fingers as he briefly studied her. She experienced his curiosity and amusement. He placed her on top of his hair. She sank into it, as if she was in a cool, bubbly ball pit. The giant continued upwards.

Bea snuggled into the giant's hair, enjoying the ride. *He's a cloud giant.* She observed the cloud steps appearing before his feet needed them. The giant reached a flickering red sky chasm as deep as sunset a few metres above them. *I wonder how many layers there are. I would like to see them all.*

Bea felt the tension the moment the giant's head and then body pulled itself through the red sky hole. Even the orange, clay-sodden earth and huge plants were alive with tremendous passion. The giant's ascent into the blood red and purple sky was slow; his clumsy footsteps were weighed down by the gravity of the landscape below him. Clouds had formed themselves into mountain landscapes of bruised purple and deep, velvet-blue undertones. The clouds burnt with a sense of injustice and anguish; she sensed the pain, hurt and terror of generations as they thundered under the weight of their experience. The giant's colour transformed to reflect the new scenery, and she understood that he too experienced the pain of the landscape.

White lightning lit up the scene to reveal expansive harvest fields below. Winged harvesters worked the fields, grabbing blackened plants from the harvest edges with large, knobbly claws and pulling with all their strength to uproot them. They flew close to the ground toward huge sky fires and tossed the weeds into them.

"Remember," said the giant, addressing her for the first time, "it is not the land that burns with injustice: it is the sky, where the light is – that's where the justice is."

She smelt the blackened disease of corruption and the oozing slime of deception seeping out of the plants. She felt the buzzing yellow malice flies eating through the weeds, and the hardened orange clay of untruth the harvesters tried to release the plants from. She felt it in her throat, like a huge ball of phlegm that would choke her.

The sky rained to empathise with the harvesters' loss and to soften the clay. The harvesters cried out to each other with painful screams at their heartache over the poor harvest, and the lightning echoed their searing loss. She experienced both their desperation and hope as they looked for small plants to save.

"Why is the harvest so full of weeds?" Bea asked the giant, feeling the ache of despair that a good harvest had been sown but not gathered.

"Greed!" said the giant with a pounding anger of thunder echoing into the clouds. "Not content with their own, they take what belongs to another."

The giant climbed higher until the purple clouds disappeared, and Bea was able to take a deep breath and swallow. The sky relaxed into pale pinks, golden slivers and grey shadows. She gazed at a pure white cloud and realised the next sky hole was in sight. Again, the giant clambered through the chasm, this time into pure white mist.

The mist was alive with a tingling brightness. It was white and pure and dwarfed everything. In the brightness, she felt an enormous, dense Presence. It enveloped her as if she was wearing it, yet it was profoundly alive and immensely aware.

"Where am I?" asked Bea insecurely.

"At the centre of everything," boomed the giant. He picked her up off his head and gently placed her in the midst of all. He bowed slowly, appreciatively acknowledging the Presence with every atom within his raindrops, and continued up.

The Presence was so intense that it was all she could do to sit down where she was. She knew again that she was truly Bea, a 12-year-old girl, and that nothing mattered. All the things that had once seemed so important flickered by briefly and disappeared forever. *The small hole in the pocket of my favourite jacket doesn't matter; or that I stole the nicer yogurts out of the fridge even when Mum hid them at the back; or my fear that I would get off the bus and my mum's usual note on the bed saying she loved me would say "goodbye" because I've been too angry, too often.*

*It doesn't matter that I've no idea what the other six universal rules are, that I've murdered a man in Vietnam when I couldn't possibly have been there, that my body is in a coma and I've no idea how to get back to it.*

Every thought vacated itself. There was nothing to think among the greatness of everything. She felt peace. The harmony of the moment, her senses finally silent, her heart quiet ... *No heartbeat*, she thought, and laughed at how much this had disturbed her. "Thank you," she said to the Presence.

She had no idea how long she was there. It seemed like moments, it could've been years. But eventually the Presence was focused on her, exploring her without judgement, but with huge affection, and it too laughed. She smiled as if her face would explode at the joy she felt in being.

"Would you like to go on an adventure?" It was the warmth of everlasting hope in its question. She felt the question pressing her skin.

"I dunno. I feel I've been on more than I can handle," Bea exclaimed.

"True," Presence said with utter truth conveyed to her unbeating heart. Presence explored her and she felt an inner globe closing inside her chest and a new warmth spreading from her heart. Presence had healed something.

"Whom shall I send?" Presence asked her spirit.

"I'm a kid," said Bea.

"You are so much more," Presence said with a truth that grew in her.

"Yes, I guess I am," she said honestly.

"I have planned good things for them: a future, freedom, hope, generosity."

She saw men in protective clothing with a quarantine emblem on their suits enter her school. They walked into her classroom and started seizing the children and staff. Scarlett was visiting from the class next door. She took one look at them and began screaming and wailing. Holly had been grabbed by a man and was fighting with arched back and had her nails in his face. Harvey ran out of the open door. Finley was hiding under the table and one of the men had hold of his leg and was dragging him out. Miss Giggle was hitting the man with a hard book. Pip was being ripped out of Miss Cotton's arms by another man; she had tears streaming down her face as she was shouting "no". The headteacher arrived. The picture faded.

Bea was stunned. Tears were flowing down her cheeks at their distress and fear. Why did the men want to take her classmates? Where were they taking them?

Presence soothed her with his interruption: "Whom shall I send?"

"Me," she said. "After all, what can they do? Being dead is so much better than being alive."

Presence smiled from the heart. "Are you dead?"

"I've never been so alive, thank you."

"You're not alone."

"No?" she asked, feeling the incredible vulnerability of a little soul in a big universe. "I killed someone."

"Yes," Presence agreed.

"And the boy died. I couldn't save him."

"Where is he now?"

She knew exactly what Presence meant – the old guy and the 10-year-old boy. They were here, of course.

"Was it a beautiful house you saw being built for him?"

"Oh yes," she said, visualising with ease the timber house she saw being built from her flight below the basket. She saw how incredibly lush the grass had been and, to her surprise, she bounced onto a field of grass with a small thud, still in her sitting position. If she'd travelled back through several Kingdom layers, she wasn't aware of it.

She was going to mourn the loss of Presence, but she became immensely aware of her surroundings. "Wow, this grass is really mossy underneath." She bounced her toes on the grass and a small purple flower appeared by her foot. It presented itself with a little shake, as if to confirm it was there. She stood up and bounced some more and a few more came up, as if their delight was to entertain her with their company. Soon she was bouncing all around the hill and small purple flowers were popping up all over the place. Bea was highly delighted.

"You don't mess about, do you?" she said to the flowers. A flower must've thought about what she said, because it changed its purple to a flourishing red and then added a small yellow band around the outer petals, and then it popped out a few similar ones, just for her pleasure. "Perfect," she said encouragingly.

"Yes, it is," said the sheep eating next to her as he nibbled on the first flower. She looked shocked. "What?" said the sheep. "Lunch is lunch, after all."

Another flower popped up between her feet, as if needing protection. "This one's mine," she said to the sheep.

"Mine," copied the sheep. "That's a nice name. I wondered what they were called." And he walked away, picking out the "Mines" and eating them as quickly as they popped up, as if they were grown for the sheep's pleasure.

She looked up. At the far end of the large field was a herd of sheep, trotting along in her direction. In the front was a sheep going at an incredible speed.

"Wow, that one is ..."

"Boundless energy," said the sheep next to her, butting in as he jogged past her to get out of Boundless's way.

*He certainly is very fast for a sheep.* Bea was contemplating his flight path. At first it seemed to be toward her, but its trajectory seemed to be something behind her. She swivelled round to see the cloud giant clambering through a sky chasm into the pasture. *Boundless is aiming for the giant; he's going to hitch a lift up the steps. What a fantastic way to get back to Presence. But the cloud steps are big – I might not make the jumps. But he's a supercharged sheep.*

The cloud giant's first step appeared, Boundless brushed by her, and she reached out with both arms, grabbed a large clump of wool and his left ear and pulled herself onto the galloping sheep. Boundless was pelting it down the field and threw himself at the first step. He quickly leapt for the second with Bea on his back.

With some effort, Boundless jumped from the second to the third step before asserting: "Aren't you supposed to ask for a lift? Can you get off now?" He refocused and leapt again.

"The steps are too far apart," she explained to Boundless. "I've got to stay on a little longer."

"Really, do you often use others like this?" explored Boundless.

"Well...". *Yes. Using my energy takes a lot of effort and other people do it better.* Which was why Bea caused a big drama when she lost anything, so her mum could spend hours looking for it, while she got on with her computer game.

"I guess that's why you're so heavy," complained the sheep.

"Are you saying that I'm fat? You're not exactly slim!"

Boundless may have been tirelessly energetic, but he had not been built to carry a Bea load while jumping metre-high, floating steps. They had hardly reached 14 metres in the air before he missed his rhythm and lost his back footing on the slippery cloud step. With Bea and his back half already off the step, his front feet slid across the cloud. Bea held on desperately to both ears as Boundless's back legs scrambled about trying to find anything solid.

"Help," shouted Boundless to the giant, who ignored him.

"Let go!" Boundless bleated to Bea, but Bea didn't want to fall, and clung on.

The last cliffhanging hoof suddenly realised that the cloud step had disappeared and Bea was desperately clinging on to Boundless's ears as the flying sheep, still sky-running, dived toward the ground and plopped through the sky hole into a new sky. Bea and Boundless descended again and, as she looked up, Bea saw the giant turn around and watch through the chasm, and she felt sure he laughed.

# 7

# Meltdown

She landed on something soft. "Ah, thank you," she sighed to Presence, only to be winded by Boundless's oversized, fat sheep body landing on top of her. "Oof, you big fat sheep!" she cried as she rolled him off her.

She glanced up at the damp, musty concrete ceiling and sat up with a swelling downheartedness; she was back in the half-light of the hospital basement. She was lying on the stinking old mattresses and feeling the gloom of life in a hospital bed dragging her down into hopeless despair.

"Oh, no! not here!" she exclaimed to Presence. There was no reply. "I can't manage this. I'm no good at it. I'm still in a coma, aren't I?" No reply. "I just want to go home." She heard an annoying chewing. She turned round to find Boundless giving himself a final shake of wool after his terrible ordeal and settling down to chew the edges of the nearest mattress.

"You're not supposed to be here," Bea explained to the sheep. "Sorry about that." She continued waiting for his "it's your fault" tirade. The sheep bleated. "Okay, I know you're mad, but you might as well say it!" she said. Boundless didn't comment but had successfully ripped into the cover of a mattress and was trying to eat its pee-ridden contents. "Don't eat that, stupid!" shouted Bea. Boundless looked up, surprised, and returned to tearing another mattress.

She tried a conversation again: "It's no good giving me the silent treatment!" She remembered her mum saying that, in many of her extended all-day mardies, followed by: "I enjoy the peace and quiet; the longer you sulk, the better it is for me."

Boundless looked at her and bleated again, as if to say: "Is this the best food you've got here. It's dreadful." "Sorry," said Bea. "Sheep don't speak here." Boundless seemed to sigh and hung his head to glare at the mattresses.

"I hope he isn't all the help I get?" she said to Presence. "Because he's just a sheep now." She couldn't feel any Presence, just the growing gloom shifting the mattresses. It was depressing.

*I don't want to be here. I'm not even home, with Mum, having tea, with my new sheep. Lettuce sandwich for you, chocolate spread on toast for me.* She pictured them sitting on the settee, watching TV.

The gloom niggled at her. *I'm here again! Which means my body is probably still on the hospital bed in a coma and Eternal will appear any minute now to drone on about destiny and dead leaders and war.*

She signalled for Boundless to follow her, but he was watching the mattresses with a long, concentrated sheep stare. "Come here, you, stupid sheep," Bea growled, as the mattress gave way beneath Boundless. With mad, crazy eyes, Boundless began to sink between the mattresses, his bottom weighing him down and his front legs slipping. Startled, Boundless twisted and turned, making it difficult for Bea to grab him. "Stop wiggling!" she cried as she seized a handful of wool, but it came loose in her hand and finally she made a desperate reach for his ear. He twitched it madly, but she held on, as her feet slipped under the mattresses.

The mattresses were separating to form a quicksand bowl and then trying to close over him. Her knees had disappeared. "We've got to get out!" she shouted to the panicking sheep, who was probably aware of this, as he was already up to his stomach in mattress. He was bolting his head backward and forward, and she was desperately hanging on when she recognised that she was up to her waist.

"Presence, help me," she muttered.

"Present?" said a familiar voice.

Eternal had entered through the door at the top of the stairs and leant on the metal rail to get a clear view of Bea's latest predicament. He was there in his favourite tight, little dark suit and bowler, with his sunglasses on. "Is that a sheep? Where did you get that?"

"Really!" said Bea, aware of the sarcasm, and that it might be a new skill she'd collected.

66

*Eternal is so annoying!* Then the added disappointment. *I really am back to being myself. Everything is irritating me again.*

"Just get me out, please," she demanded.

"It's your adventure," he sighed self-righteously, looking up at the ceiling.

She was sinking to her armpits and Boundless was a head in a bed. Bea ached for Presence and the strange kingdom that seemed a million miles away. Boundless interrupted with a bleat. *All I've got left is the sheep. Well, its nose.* She gripped his ear a little tighter and he bleated in pain.

"You've had plenty of time to think of a universal rule to break as you lay dying of Yancy's well-aimed bullet." Eternal clarified, "That was rule number four, by the way: death. The rhythm of life; nothing is permanent."

Bea did in fact have a universal rule up her sleeve, but she was trying to work out how to use it. *Cause and effect – there's a relationship between me receiving a bullet and someone shooting me. But how do you break the rule? And it's got to get rid of the gloomy mattresses too. I could burn the mattresses, and hope we don't end up being Guy Fawkes and lamb chops in a bonfire. But if it goes wrong? I need more time.*

Boundless had disappeared altogether into the mattress bog, and Bea's chin rested on a stinky mattress. She looked like a single Brussels sprout on top of a pile of meat.

"How was it for you, reincarnation? Escaping the inescapable?" Eternal queried.

"Now is not the time!" scowled Bea. *I'm not sharing it with you, 'smug-pants Eternal'.*

*I've only been in this old, out-of-body life for five minutes and I'm up to my neck in it! Why is everything so difficult here? I just want to go home. If I let go, maybe there will be a little house for me? What kind of place would that be?*

Bea was giving in. Boundless had stopped moving under the weight of mattress, which wasn't a good sign. *The sheep's dead, Eternal's gloating, Presence isn't here and I'm up to my eyes in it, on my own. He said I wouldn't be alone. Surely he doesn't mean Eternal's here to help me? Then why isn't he helping? I want my mum!*

She felt like a small and overwhelmed little person as the mattresses crept over her head, stifling the air. "If I could think of something, I would say it!" she muffled.

Despite the mattress earmuffs, Bea heard Eternal as clear as a bell, saying quite distinctly: "Rule five: the law of mind. Thought precedes action." Eternal replied, "So, they say."

The sunshine was making a half-hearted effort to light up the room, as Bea lifted her head from the mattress it was lying on, to find her own body taking up most of the bed. It looked peaceful, her mother was sitting on the bed, stroking Bea's hair, where the bandage had once been. At that moment, in Bea's eyes, her mum was the most beautiful person she'd ever seen. A tired woman, with too many worry wrinkles for her age, and a ridiculous passion for colourful patterned clothes. She was patience and calmness in the storms of life; she was an endless cuddle regardless of whether you deserved one; she was the joy of a face you might never see again; she was love. Bea flung her arms around her mum and gasped tears of gratitude. Flooding out of her came the ache of knowing that she hadn't recognised the huge love her mum gave her, just by being there, day after day. She had not related well.

Bea sobbed. "I'm sorry. I should've found a way to let you know that I love you being my mum." She cried and rubbed her snot on her mum's summer dress.

Her mum did not feel the hug or the dampness of Bea, but she sensed her daughter was trying to say something. She picked up her daughter's hand from the body lying on the hospital bed.

Her mum spoke to Bea's body, "I can feel you. Isn't that ridiculous, but I've always known when you were around. I miss you peeping at me, Bea, from the corner of your eyes."

Her mum put her hand to her mouth to stifle the moans, but it was too late – the tears were leaking out.

"Come back to me, honey. Just hang on, okay? They're going to try something, something very new, a new procedure, you've just got to hold on, okay?" She choked on the words, "They say you'll come back to me, if it works, and you'll be better. Better? Can you believe it!"

Bea stopped her sniffling and wiped her tears on her pyjama top and looked at her mum. "What new procedure?"

"You just got to hang on, honey. You'll be able to say, 'I love you mum'," she said, tears rolling down her cheeks.

"Is this about you feeling lonely?" said Bea. "What procedure? What's happening?"

"You'll know I've always loved you, Bea. Even if I had to get you to do things you didn't want to, well that's pretty much everything, isn't it?"

"Are you starting that again!" cried Bea. "You always ruin the moment."

"You'll look at me Bea and have a chat over a coffee. You'll grow up. Imagine. You'll ask for a chip butty; you might even eat beans! They say it could change your autism completely!" Her mum smiled through the tears.

Bea reeled from the revelation. *I'm autistic! How could I have forgotten? I'm autistic! I can't even speak properly! I say phrases from my favourite cartoons. "You're a stink-bomb, sucker!" "Read it and weep, sly-boy." "It really hurt and then some." I can't express my thoughts in words!*

*I'm autistic! How could I forget that! My thoughts don't register in an order. I can't identify feelings until I've spent ages processing them! I struggle to order information, it all sits on the edge of my mouth and refuses to come out. Then it ram-raids its way out in short, grumpy incoherent, random words. I can read people, but I don't get why they are the way they are. I've always been autistic! How could I forget something like that?*

*But outside my body, my brain can act like a superspeed highway? Everything is clear and logical and there's order and it's sharper than lemon. I'm using words I must've heard somewhere and never registered. Like 'registered'. I can visualise memories, plan for the future, take out distractions. I have focus.*

*My brain works better outside of my body. I don't need a procedure to do this – I'm doing it! But what if I go back into my body and I can't talk?* Bea panicked. *I'll get frustrated because I want to say, "What the hell are you doing, Mum? What if I can't think anything at all? What if I'm brain dead..."*

Bea realised Boundless had survived the mattress swamp and followed her into the ward. Now he was chewing something at the end of the bed. It looked suspiciously like her medical notes!

"No," shouted Bea. "I need them. I need to see what's going on, you stupid, stupid sheep!"

She hit Boundless away from the notes. He looked slightly offended, but there was no way Bea's slaps were going to penetrate that woolly coat. Her hands bounced off as if that was exactly why he'd put a woolly coat on. Boundless refused to give back the last little bit of writing and trotted off around the room to nibble it in peace.

As if on cue, two nurses appeared with a trolley. "Hello Mrs Tanner. We'll just get Bea ready for theatre. We're going to add another drip feed to her other arm for the anaesthetic."

"Over my dead body!" said Bea. "No, no, wait," shouted Bea, leaping to defend her body.

The nurses continued their preparations while Bea's mum held her body's hand.

"The surgeon is waiting for her. It'll be at least four hours and they'll give her time to come out of it naturally," said the overweight nurse puffing her way around the bed.

"Don't just sit there and let this happen! What if it doesn't work? What if I'm worse?"

"She might be sitting up by tea time," encouraged the tiny, chirpy nurse.

"She might not!" shouted Bea.

She twisted back towards her mum. "Why would you want this? What if I spend my life scrolling celebrity gossip and cute puppies and bitching about the kids in my class, like my cousins do! They're the ones without brains!" said Bea as her voice gained momentum.

"Are you going to the canteen or home?" asked the big nurse.

"Why? Do you want to go to the canteen too? You huge, fat, body-stealing ...". Bea was rolling nicely over into abusive language and enjoying the fact it could now come out of her mouth.

Boundless was glaring suspiciously at the mattress. He bit it, waiting to see if it would grab him. He backed off and then moved forward and bit it again.

The nurse asked her mum to hold Bea's hair and began to shave the side of her head.

"My hair! How dare you touch it! Get off me! Get off me now before I hit you." Bea tried to grab the electric trimmer but the nurse had a firm grip. "Give that to me, you hair-stealing ...". She slapped the nurse, but the nurse felt nothing and continued her shaving.

Bea rounded on her mum, drawing close to her face, "What have you agreed to?"

Bea felt the hot swell of a meltdown pressing through from the back of her head to her eyes. "I'm not going to be different so we can have coffee together and say I love you! I don't love you! Yes, I do, but I don't! I'm autistic! I'm not normal! Don't you dare make me normal! And I'm never, never eating beans! You can't make me!"

She turned back to the large nurse. "Give me my hair back," she said, snatching the bits of hair that fell to the floor anyway. "And my body! Get off it! Get off me! That's me!"

Eternal appeared in a surgery gown, cap and gloves. His glasses were off and the shapes in his eyes were as green as the gown.

"Yes! I'm ready to break a rule," she said with dark, menacing undertones. "You knew I was autistic, you little ... you're not a surgeon! You stupid being! Stop dressing up in silly clothes! I'm not five! Why didn't you tell me I was autistic! They're going to make me a zombie. They're going to change me!" Bea was hyperventilating.

"Bea, don't you like talking and speaking in a more lucid and organised fashion?" said Eternal, helpfully.

"No, no! No! No! No! I just want to be me! I want to be me!" Bea grew herself up to her full anger and screamed, throwing down her fists on the end of the bed, her anger reverberating into the room like a massive explosion of feeling. A syringe teetering on the edge of the trolley tinkled to the floor. It wasn't much of a reaction for such a massive feeling. The nurse lunged for it and missed.

"I'll have to get another syringe!" she exclaimed to the chirpy one, as she popped out of the door.

"They're doing a nice fish pie in the canteen today," the small nurse bubbled.

"Breathe, Bea," said Eternal in a calming and slightly patronising voice.

"My body's on the bed with some of its hair missing!" growled Bea. "Tell that to breathe!"

Bea was past the explosion, but her loss had nowhere to go and she felt as if her insides were spilling out on the floor.

Eternal tried to hold ground under the storm of feeling: "You will be yourself. Just a more constructive ..."

Bea stormed at Eternal: "I'd stuff that tube down your mouth if I thought it'd shut you up!" She pointed her finger at his tirelessly smug face. "I am not changing! I am not! I am not!" she screamed. Bea's feelings were spilling into every crevice of her senses, and still she couldn't get them out.

She dropped to her knees, tears rolling down her eyes, and begged her mum, "Don't let them do this to me."

Boundless ambled over to her and she sank her head into his wool and sobbed. He nuzzled her with his big sheep head; but it was a disguised head butt. "Ow!" she said.

Eternal was looking at the sheep suspiciously. "Where did the sheep come from?"

"This is my sheep!" Bea muttered. "No one is taking the sheep or me!" she said, rubbing her nose and grabbing his ear to prevent him headbutting her again.

That's when the light came on. Bea paused her grief. *Eternal doesn't know where I went after I left Vietnam. If Eternal is eternal, how come he doesn't know?* She stopped crying. *I've been through Vietnam; I know how to get to the super-calm highway in my head. I don't need to lose myself in a huge tantrum –it doesn't achieve the result I want.* Her emotions drained away, as if they were on the end of a large, high-quality syringe. Her calm appeared under her red eyes and she stood up and looked Eternal squarely in the face.

"Don't you know where Boundless comes from?" she said, indicating to the sheep with a scowl.

"I'm universal, not personal," said Eternal calmly, but with a slightly irritated undertone.

"That's why you don't get me," said Bea calmly.

Her thinking was shifting, and Eternal could see a flicker of suspicion pass over her face. *The universe is incredibly personal; I've seen it. The Kingdom is about as personal as you can get.*

"It's time to let the sheep go, Bea," said Eternal gently.

"Nope. Time to break a rule," said Bea, watching him closely.

"It's a figment of your imagination" explained Eternal, "a woolly comfort blanket."

"You don't get to tell me what I do," Bea said, keeping one eye on the nurses and their preparations as they reassured her mum. *Before they operate, I've got to steal my body back.*

Eternal squared up to Bea. It was time she saw the reality of the situation.

"You killed a man. A man's life is worth several sheep, you can let it go. It's not like you have a passion for pets," he said, calmly allowing the words to drift into her as he paused to measure the reaction. "You are autistic; you just needed time and space to remember it." Another pause. Bea remembered.

"Autistic people don't relate easily to others, but you lack any empathy at all. It's not in your makeup. Some autistic people have it. You don't." Eternal knew acceptance was the key to change.

Bea flicked her eyes away, as if thinking, and took in the nurses who had completed their preparations.

Eternal wasn't getting through, so he moved up a gear: "You are completely self-focused and ruthlessly pursue what you need and want. You would make a good hired killer, but your anti-authoritarian attitude makes you dangerous."

*To whom?* thought Bea, impressing herself with the correct grammar.

Eternal continued the attack: "When you pulled the trigger on Morales, you gained endorphin pleasure from it. It gave you a high!"

*Yes, that's true, but how did you know that, Eternal?*

Eternal knew he'd captured Bea's attention. "In the same way, when you manipulate your mother to do what you want, by threatening a meltdown, you get pleasure from it."

He was aiming for a reaction. Bea felt a welling emotion, but sidelined it; it wasn't important.

Eternal went in for the 'kill': "You need this operation, because you are a psychopath waiting to happen."

"Everyone is always telling me who I am," she replied, thinking of Yancy.

"Each person has a window of themselves that they can't see, but other people can," said Eternal, pleased by the dialogue and the reduction in emotion. "This operation will give you cognitive abilities, so you can manage your emotions and the psychopath in you."

The nurses rolled Bea's body carefully onto a trolley and rearranged it into a relaxed pose.

Eternal softened his voice, "You think just because you're not in Vietnam you aren't capable of repeating murder in a different, stressful situation? Did you want to kill Yancy too?" He extended his hand towards her, offering her the support she desperately wanted through the stress of change. "You've got a taste for it and you know you will."

Bea had let him talk; she wanted to understand the agenda behind the ethereal being. At the same time, she had watched Boundless squeeze his big sheep butt under the hospital trolley her body was lying on. She saw the larger nurse open the door as the chirpy one wheeled the unmanageable and tightly squeezed sheep trolley out of the door.

"Think about it, Bea," said Eternal. "You know I'm right. You don't recognise how intentional and purposeful you will become after this small operation."

"Bye," said Bea, diving for the door and running through it, just as Boundless picked up speed under the trolley. The nurses were stunned as the trolley bounded forward and hurtled off by itself down the corridor. They didn't see Bea running after the hijacked sheep trolley shouting, "Boundless, you're an amazing friend and a genius sheep." No one saw Boundless smile.

# 8

## Tea and biscuits

The hefty nurse had given up, about five strides into the corridor chase, leaving the tiny nurse to pursue the runaway trolley. Bea watched the lift doors shut and knew the only option left was the stairs. Bea was aiming for the basement. It was the only place she could think of – they'd never make it through a car park of security and people.

She pulled her body off the trolley. *I should be lighter than this; I'm only eating through a tube!*

Boundless tried to exit his position under the trolley. Unfortunately, he was stuck. It had been one thing to squeeze under the trolley, but when he tried to squeeze out, the trolley stayed attached.

Bea pulled her body through the stair doors, the pee bag fell off and got stuck in the door. The contents spilt out as she slipped on her pee tube and descended the stairs on her back, legs akimbo, her arms tightly clinging to her body. *This is going to hurt*, she thought, but it didn't, well not to her consciousness, anyway, as she rattled down half the stairs before landing in a heap. Her body's nose definitely looked broken.

"Good job you're in a coma, Bea," she said to her unconscious self.

Boundless had failed to extract himself from the trolley and decided to hurtle himself through the door after Bea, rather than be left behind. He too was now plunging down the stairs in his trolley regalia. He had picked up too much speed as the trolley momentum had got the better of him, his hooves left the floor and the trolley collided with the banister railing. Bea heard the noise before she saw the caged sheep, leaving just enough time to brace herself for impact and lie as flat as possible. Boundless flew over Bea's head, bounced off the stairwell wall and its banister and carried on around the corner and down another set of steps, bleating and gathering speed as gravity took over. She heard him clattering and bashing down a third set of steps before, with an

76

almighty smash, she realised he'd made it to the bottom. Not all the trolley bits had, and an occasional clink-ting of minor metal pieces tinkered their way gently down the stairs.

The chirpy nurse waited at the lift with a security guard, watching the numbers going up and down, oblivious.

Bea listened to see if she could hear Boundless. It was very quiet. "You okay?" she whispered. No reply. "Boundless?" she called. She heard an annoyed, grumbled bleat at the bottom of the stairs. "At least you've got a coat to absorb some of the bruises."

She exhaled her emotions, stood up and tentatively picked up the remains of the pee tube. She bumped her body slowly and carefully down the steps. The wet parts left a slimy trail, but she knew they'd soon dry in the warm hospital atmosphere. It was difficult to get the body past the trolley fragments and one or two more tinkled down the steps.

At the bottom, Boundless was free of metal and standing by the door waiting to escape his bobsleigh experience. He was holding his leg up.

*Oh no!* thought Bea. She pushed the sheep aside to open the door and watched him limp down the corridor. *Bruised, not broken*, she deduced.

The corridor was clear, so she dragged her saggy body down toward the basement door.

Boundless entered first and trot-limped down the metal stairs, while Bea bumped her bruised and battered body down the final steps. "You'll thank me one day, I think," she told her body.

Boundless was doing his best sheep growl to the mattresses near the bottom of the stairs. It was more of a bleat really, with a throaty gesture at the end. This was clearly a sheep on the edge, because the mattresses seemed to understand "I will eat you all" in sheep bleat and were slipping slowly back, leaving enough room for Bea to drag the body toward the cleaner's table. *Maybe Boundless is going to be a bigger help than I thought.*

Bea dragged her body onto a chair, but it refused to sit down and slipped off. She sighed, pulled her torso onto one chair, and put her feet on another one, and leant it towards the table. *It's not doing well. It has a broken nose, a burst pee bag and no monitor to tell if it's still alive.* She tidied up her operation gown and made her body a cup of tea from the flask in a dirty cup. *In case it should wake. Not that I drink tea, but it looks like I care. See, I'm not a psychopath. Not to myself, anyway.*

She sat down on the last cleaner's chair, looking at the mess of herself and Boundless. "I've kidnapped my own body," she said to Boundless. The mattresses were watchful, and already she felt the dull pressure of hopelessness. "I need some answers." Boundless did his best to look like an intelligent, listening sheep, but his foot was sore and he was hungry, so he sniffled at the biscuits on the table.

"Okay," she said, untwisting the packet of digestives and feeding Boundless a biscuit. "I'm autistic, but I'm changing. Being able to talk helps you to think clearer. I know you can't at the moment, sorry, I'm not rubbing it in. Is that empathy? I don't think so. Have another biscuit." Boundless liked the digestives.

"We're not in danger. We can think. Think! Let's start with the easy stuff," Bea explained to a crunching Boundless. "Some things are piecing together. Others aren't."

"There are nine rules and I've used five: gravity attracts, history repeats, gender, death, mind precedes action. They're all universal rules. We like to think before we act, but do we always? We all die, except do we really? You would know that one," she reminded Boundless. "We all have gravity, but we defy it; history repeats, but not always, not indefinitely. We all have a gender, or a mixed-up one, like snails.

"So, I need to know the final four. I think I know two, but I can't say it, in case," she whispered, "he comes in."

She continued to whisper to the nuzzling Boundless, "What does Eternal get if I break these rules? What's in my destiny that he's after?" She lowered her voice further. "If he's Eternal, he should know everything. So, how come he didn't know where you came from? What's he really about, eh? What happens after I've broken the ninth rule?"

She offered Boundless tea from her body's cup and he slurped at it.

"Are you drinking from your nose?" she asked, watching the brown drips run out of his nostrils and onto the floor.

"Moving on. Why did I go to Vietnam? To rescue my grandad from killing his superior? Who's to say he wouldn't have met Milton rather than Yancy, anyway? And what about the world order that's manipulated the world by killing off any leader it disagrees with and replacing it with another war-hungry one, so it can create financial progress. Why is that important? I can't stop it?"

She got Boundless's attention away from the mattresses he was growl-bleating at by dangling a biscuit under his nose.

"Pay attention," she said, then laughed as she said it, because she'd never paid attention to anyone who said "pay attention".

*What is that?* she thought.

"Wow, I'm laughing at me; I never laugh at me," she snorted as she held Boundless's face between her hands, and in a moment of unexpected joy at herself, she gave him a hug.

"Okay, back to big thoughts," she said, forgetting to whisper. "What is Eternal not telling me? He's all secrets, really, isn't he?"

The gloom was deepening and the mattresses were edging forwards. Thinking was getting hard work.

"How can we protect my body? Someone will find it soon, if the gloom-mongers don't get it?" she said, nodding to the mattresses. Boundless hung his head and gave them another growl-bleat. He hadn't forgotten being suffocated.

"Last biscuit; you'll be fat. Listen, Boundless, I'm turning into my mother! I'm changing! I'm feeding a sheep biscuits. I told my mum I loved her. Okay and I said I didn't love her too. I feel different inside," she said, touching her warm heart. "Did you know you slobber when you eat?" Again, she caught herself sounding grown up and laughed.

Her clear thinking was going. "I don't have any answers. What do you do if you don't have answers?"

She looked at Boundless, "Eating isn't the answer." She laughed, wrapping up the small number of uneaten biscuits and popping them into her body's hand in case it woke up.

"We have to see this through, buddy," she told him, braving herself and patting him on the head. She stood up to pace about.

"I can't get back in my body without knowing my destiny and purpose." She turned. "Vietnam obviously didn't tell me all of it, only the history." She spun again, "I need to break a rule and find out what is really happening now, at this moment. Hey! This pacing is really helpful."

Eternal walked through the wall nearest the table. He was dressed like an old-fashioned teacher with a mortar board and gown on and a small cane in his hand that he was wafting about. His glasses were in a little pocket in the gown, his eyes a matching dark purple glinting through the light in his eyes.

*You're not my teacher*, she thought, *but I need answers.*

"I need to find out what's really happening." She grasped the moment: "Why do you need me to break rules? What are you not telling me about? Why do you think you're my teacher? I'm autistic? But, I'm not stupid."

He seemed pleased at all the questions and the fact that, again, Bea had reached a state of lucid reasoning and wasn't a fireball of emotions. "I see you are ready to break a rule," he stated conceitedly.

"Yes, of course. It seems to be the only way to get answers. I just want an answer to my question. What do you get out of this? Apart from being excessively coordinated?"

"Enabling you to fulfil your purpose, is my purpose." He paused, admiring his new outfit, "You think so? Excellent vocabulary you're using."

"I know," said Bea, not wanting to get side-tracked, "but what is my purpose?"

"You will know that when you've completed the ninth rule," said Eternal, helpfully.

"Is my purpose good?"

"It is powerful. Good is a judgement call you will be able to make before you break your ninth universal rule."

"Why do you want me to have the operation?" asked Bea with open suspicion.

"So you live, or else this journey of ours is for nothing."

"Will I live?"

"Yes, well," said Eternal, "with a perceptive and astute mind." He answered, anticipating her concern.

"Will I speak?"

Eternal expressed warmth at such a simple request: "Concisely and clearly."

"Why Vietnam?"

"You chose the doors," said Eternal, shrugging his large, gowned shoulders. "Want to know more?" He gestured to a door that had appeared where he came from.

"Can you keep my body safe until I get back?"

"Your body has always been safe," replied Eternal, ethereally. "Ready to break a rule?" He took his glasses out of his pocket and opened his hands in a welcoming manner.

"Boundless," she shouted to the sheep, and Boundless obediently came to her.

"Impressive," said Eternal. "You seem to have gained animal training skills."

"Biscuits," said Bea. She didn't want Eternal focusing on Boundless in case the sheep was a deal-breaker. She knew she had to go through the next door, so she replied quickly: "Why isn't time a universal rule?"

"Because it isn't constant."

"So, there must be a way to move through space and matter, just like time. Because that can't be constant either."

"Impressive reasoning," Eternal congratulated his pupil. "Everything vibrates, therefore you can pass through it."

"Rule six: Vibration. Three to complete," said Eternal with pleasure.

Eternal twisted his neck around under his thick, starched collar as his gaze focused on a door until it swung open.

Bea took a reluctant look at her body, before gripping Boundless's ear and running for the open door.

Half an hour later, two cleaners appeared on the metal steps. They were surprised to see the body of a battered young girl sitting at their table by herself. It seemed she had woken briefly to eat their biscuits and drink their tea before going back into a deep coma.

# 9

## Rosie the robot

Bea was very uncomfortable. There was a shelf above her neck, so her chin rested on her chest and a big sheep's butt squashed her against the wall. "This is not really space!" she muttered to Eternal. No reply.

The cupboard door opened and a plump woman's body with the palest arms leant over the shelving to grab sticky tape. Behind her warm olive smock with big yellow flowers, a familiar face peeped around to swipe a confiscated tub of playdough: Ralphy. He looked intently into her eyes, his head tilted on one side, as if he saw everything she was. He gave her a big smile. "57," said Ralphy, happily.

Bea noticed Ralphy as if for the first time. He was full of Presence, as if it radiated from him like sunshine. Why had she never seen it before?

"Out of the cupboard," Miss Cotton said to Ralphy. She manoeuvred her perfectly sized bottom to block Ralphy from entering the cupboard. "What've you got?" she laughed as she turned around to catch him. He escaped across the classroom to eat playdough.

"Miss Cotton!" exclaimed Bea, delighted to see her teacher. She dived to hug Miss Cotton's squidgy waist, smelling her rose deodorant and long, chestnut hair. Miss Cotton showed no recognition of Bea or her clinging hug, effortlessly removing herself. "Make good choices, Ralphy; give me the playdough."

Boundless took the opportunity to escape the cupboard and explore the bright, warm, spacious classroom. He shook his wool until the dust sprinkled. Harvey spotted the dust particles in the sunlight and tried to catch them as if they were bubbles.

Bea beamed with happiness at the familiar scene. *Miss Cotton's class is the safest place I know, apart from my own bed. Here every little success is a big celebration. It's fun, chaos and it's also writing.*

"Miss Cotton!" Bea shouted. Miss Cotton, oblivious, headed across the classroom to mend the book Pip had just ripped.

There were seven children between the ages of 6 and 12. They were all pre-verbal autistic with limited, if any, speech. Bea was the eldest. She was supposed to have moved to the 'Annex' at the other end of the playground. It held two secondary school classes for pre-verbal autistic children, but each time they took her to visit, she spreadeagled herself in the doorway. Miss Cotton reluctantly agreed that Bea wasn't quite ready for the transition. As a result, each week, Miss Giggle walked her across the playground to "visit" the annex door, in the hope she would choose to go in.

The white board at the front of the room showed colourful floating bubbles and played calming music. On top of the whiteboard, a phone was precariously balanced to stop Finley dismantling it. There were several workstations around the classroom to encourage writing, motor skills and construction, and a sensory area with spinners and rockers to soothe the heightened senses down. In the centre of the room there were two tables, where a lot of snacking and lunch happened.

Miss Giggle, the TA, was hugging Pip and readjusting his ear defenders. He had been over-sensitised by her rendition of 'Five Little Speckled Frogs'. Holly was writing a list of the items in her sandwich box. Boundless was eating the last list.

Harvey was snuggling into the big sheep's wool. If anyone could give Boundless a race it would be Harvey; he was very agile. When Harvey wasn't spaced out, he was escaping. Miss Cotton had their only bookshelf dismantled after Harvey climbed up it, detached the polystyrene tiles and entered the attic of electrics. It took the two caretakers and headteacher at least an hour to find and extract him.

Wyatt was watching the laptop's rendition of floating bubbles. He stopped drawing on the paper and chose to draw on the laptop instead. The walls had scrubbed smudges all over them from some of his previous masterpieces. At the top of the walls, laminated pictures encouraged phonics and number patterns. This stopped Ralphy eating the Blu Tack and Wyatt drawing over them. The class had a feeling of space, yet there seemed to be too much activity to hold it.

Bea remembered the times she'd spent in the classroom as Miss Cotton patiently taught her to order letters and numbers, add and subtract, thump the floor and not another kid, even if they were intensely irritating. She relived the moments Miss Cotton took her clothes to the hand dryer because there was a wet spot, and removed vegetables someone had put on her plate. How she had wrapped her arms around her as she went into meltdown and rocked her until she came out of it. She was a good teacher. Bea appreciated it. She felt it in her heart – a connection that moved her toward an unusual emotion she couldn't identify.

Bea surveyed her familiar classroom through the eyes of her recent experiences. *The tables and chairs are ridiculously small. I know all the books and toys, the timetabled routine, the other kids flapping and stimming. I know how intense their senses are, but when I'm calm, my mind is crystal clear. This classroom is all I've known. It's the constant in my life, but weirdly, today, I can see I've outgrown it. Presence is right, I'm more than this now.* For the first time Bea hesitated; *maybe I don't want to be autistic any more.*

Ralphy had gone back to matching a number puzzle. She walked over to him. He looked up to smile and then refocused. *How come Ralphy and Harvey can see us, but Miss Cotton can't? Of course, Boundless is full of Presence and so is Ralphy; maybe Ralphy sees Presence in me. After all, I've spent time there, and Presence healed my heart.*

Miss Cotton took Finley over to have his hand painted. Bea admired Miss Cotton's bravery and persistence. *Finley hates anything sticky.* Finley looked disgusted at the thought of the paint and tried to make a run for it. Miss Cotton had a firm grip around his waist and was talking quietly to him as she dipped his hand in the gloop! She pressed it onto the love heart of pink hands that made up a large card. The inside of the heart read: "To Bea, we miss you, get well soon xx".

*Do they miss me?* thought Bea. Miss Cotton was still holding a shaking Finley, whose hand was pressed down onto a second card. "To Morgan, we miss you, get well soon xx". *Oh, it's a standard message. Where is Morgan?* She looked around the classroom. *He must've been in the accident too.*

Bea leant into Ralphy's face, "Where's Morgan?"

Ralphy looked up from number 92 of the matching game, and pointed to the cupboard.

"He's in the cupboard?" Bea asked. "He's where I am? In the hospital! Of course!"

The door beeped. Everyone looked up. A man stood at the door, and in front of him a child-sized robot slid into the room. Harvey made a dart for the corridor door, and the robot man slid to the side and, with a practised hand, shut the door quickly.

The robot was familiar, it had been coming to school every Thursday for several weeks. It aimed to encourage communication by repeating the children's phrases. It was brightly coloured, with big, googly eyes and a metal smile that was more real than the man's smile. The robot man was anxious around kids, so he spent his time talking to Miss Giggle and typing on his laptop.

Boundless had moved next to Bea in a protective stance and was also assessing the man. His jumper had a bobbly, textured pattern. "That's never a good thing," Bea whispered to Boundless. "Yes, that's your wool he's wearing."

The pupils sensory state rapidly escalated. Ralphy squealed "9,9,9" and banged his head on the table. Pip jumped into Miss Giggle's arms for protection and began rocking. Harvey darted around the room looking for an escape hatch. Finley dived under a table, spreading the painted hand marks with him, found a bolt and unscrewed it. Wyatt was more confrontational; he took his felt tip over to the robot and tried to stab it. As if sensing the danger, the robot kept moving back, closer to its owner, until it was pinned against the door.

"Please don't do that; it's very expensive," Bobbly man snivelled.

"You need to ask reception to phone through before entering!" Miss Cotton said sternly, opening the door at the other end of the room to the playground with Holly attached to her smock. Ralphy made a bolt for it along with a barefoot Harvey, Pip in his socks and Finley with the table bolt in his mouth.

Miss Cotton was cross: "It's not a good time. Three of our children were in a minibus crash and the class are still traumatised! Would it be possible to come back another day? With notice!"

Bobbly man was not impressed with this idea. He had deadlines and the headteacher's permission.

Bea tuned out of the argument. *I'm injured, Morgan is injured, Pip sits on the school bus but he's back at school, hard to tell if he's okay he's always traumatised. Maybe Morgan is conscious and he'll remember the crash? I have to find him. Not that I get on with Morgan. I'm autistic, I don't get on with anyone, just particularly not Morgan.*

Bea wasn't used to bothering with adult conversations and found it difficult to concentrate on this one.

Miss Cotton was not letting up: "Mr Orme, your company might be sponsoring the new playground equipment, but these children are traumatised and now's not a good time!"

"I only have three weeks to complete the study. I'm on a deadline. The university is waiting on the research, as is the company. We have a legal, signed agreement with your headteacher," Mr Orme protested.

Miss Cotton looked uncertain, "Just go sit at the corner table, but Bea and Morgan aren't here, and the others may not want to engage with your robot. They're highly sensitised today!" Miss Cotton shook her head in annoyance.

*Of course, the problem isn't the toy – it's the man watching; none of us like being watched.* Bea and Morgan were the eldest, and the most confident. They had been given the chance to work with the robot first. She'd enjoyed hearing Rosie the robot repeat, "Wipe my pants with a toothbrush!"

Bea wasn't as fluent as Morgan and had found her lack of connecting phrases totally frustrating, especially if she wanted a variation, like "Yes, I want cake, but not that one!" Morgan managed to say small sentences like "another choice please" and, when she got jealous about it, she'd thump him. But Morgan couldn't think of what to say to the robot and just kept saying "Hello robot", which delighted Bea.

"Keep the playground door open and bring Finley in, will you Miss Giggle?" Miss Cotton instructed. Miss Giggle looked at the robot and smiled as she raised her eyebrows to Miss Cotton, but Bea didn't understand what the communication meant.

Miss Giggle was a young, curvaceous, doe-eyed teaching assistant with a thick scoop of make-up on. Bea recognised there was a teacher hierarchy she'd previously been unaware of.

Miss Giggle dragged the reluctant Finley through the door and pointed to the robot. Finley's face lit up and he ran towards it.

"This is Finley. He likes mechanical things," Miss Giggle explained.

"Hello Finley," said Mr Orme in his best inoffensive voice. "Have you come to see Rosie the robot?"

Finley gave no recognition of Mr Orme. Finley held the robot's shoulders and drew his eyes close to its eyes.

"Gently," said Miss Giggle to Finley.

Finley turned around to think into space. He grinned at Bea. She was impressed he had seen her; Finley rarely made eye contact, but his eyes were alive with mischief. Finley was examining the last of the paint on his hand, and licking it off. His other hand was fiddling with the robot.

Orme explained to Miss Giggle that Finley just needed to say something to the robot.

"The children are pre-verbal autistic." Miss Giggle was exasperated. "Finley only makes sounds and not to order. You'll just have to wait."

Finley threw something onto the floor. Bea went over to get a closer look and Boundless followed. It was a sticker with a logo she'd seen in Vietnam.

*How's this connected? Why's this company sponsoring our playground equipment?*

Finley found a wire under the robot's elbow and pulled it out, shouting a triumphant "Eee".

Rosie the robot mimicked him: "Eeee!" as its arm went limp.

Mr Orme looked horrified at the expensive robot arm. Miss Giggle asked if he'd finished with Finley and, apparently, he had. Miss Cotton watched, smiling her secret I've-just-nibbled-on-a-chocolate-from-my-bag smile.

Finley refused to be taken outside and sat on a table contemplating the robot. Miss Cotton purposefully ignored him and stood by the playground door talking to Miss Giggle. Bea never paid attention to the antics of other children, and hadn't realised how entertaining it could be. Now she watched the unfolding drama with delight.

Mr Orme looked edgily at Finley as he laid Rosie on the table and took out a small toolkit from his pocket. He was saying things under his breath. Finley was focused on the toolkit and how the robot arm opened. Mr Orme turned his back on Finley, so Finley dragged a chair nearer and watched.

*Ha! Now you know what it's like to be stared at.*

Mr Orme was getting flustered and trying to get the teacher's attention, but they were focused on the playground.

"71," said a voice behind her. Ralphy was peering suspiciously at Orme.

Orme was feeling the pressure: "Move along," he said to Ralphy.

Ralphy stared into Bea's eyes as he squatted down and opened the man's displaced laptop, discarded on the floor. She smiled at Ralphy.

"We need Arthur," she whispered.

Arthur was a computer whizz. He had hacked into the school system last year just to wish everyone a happy Christmas. It took the experts three weeks and a complete reboot to get rid of it, so he wasn't allowed on the school laptops, officially. Unfortunately, Arthur was in the classroom on the other side of the corridor and both doors needed a fob to access them.

Bea assessed the situation. *I might be able to vibrate through the door, but Arthur wouldn't. On the good side, I'm invisible and might be able to steal a fob, if I waited long enough for a teacher to bend down. I don't have much time. Mr Orme might leave, or pick up the laptop. I could break a rule? I need some chaos.* "Cause and effect," she said.

Eternal appeared on the whiteboard.

"Some things begin small but have larger consequences?" said Eternal, helpfully.

"Yes, the butterfly effect!" said Bea.

"Cause and effect. Rule number seven. Two to complete," exclaimed Eternal, disappearing.

As if in slow motion, Bea watched Ralphy put a small computer chip Orme had left on the table into his mouth. Ralphy chewed and choked. Miss Cotton heard the familiar sound first and came running toward him to do the Heimlich manoeuvre. She grabbed him from behind and did a well-rehearsed press to the chest.

*She really is a fantastic teacher*, Bea thought, as the chip darted across the room to hit Holly squarely in the eye. Miss Cotton looked horrified as Holly let out a huge yowl of protest and started screaming. At which point, Finley picked up the chip and skipped outside. Orme was clearly distraught, shouting about "thousands of pounds" as he ran after Finley, who was delighted by the game. Bea, thrilled by the opportunity, snatched Orme's fob as he ran by. She hurried towards the internal door, closely followed by Boundless and Harvey.

Outside the corridor, she stopped. *I've always wanted one of these*, she thought, picturing all the interesting doors she could access: the science cupboard, the staff room. *Ooh, it was so tempting.*

Boundless nudged her hand.

"Okay," she groaned, "let's get Arthur."

She entered Miss Thompson's classroom and, before she could shut the door, Harvey and Boundless dived in. Harvey, heading for freedom, seized the fob off Bea, and while Miss Thompson was still trying to work out what Harvey was doing in her class, he was out of the playground door, through the gate and heading for a large sycamore tree. The chaos continued as Miss Thompson, the caretaker and his ladder, and finally Miss Cotton, tried to peel Harvey from a branch of the tree.

Most of the class watched, except Arthur, who believed Harvey's antics to be slapstick and beneath him. He was stimming absent-mindedly with a fidget toy, spinning it around in his fingers.

This gave Bea enough time to scribble on a piece of paper: "We need you now! love from Ralphy" and shove it in front of Arthur. She was just contemplating how to get Arthur out of the room when Arthur walked to the door, checked no one was watching, pressed his phone against the fob pad and opened it.

*Well*, thought Bea, *he's a genius!*

Ralphy gave a deep smile from his eyes, as Bea and Arthur walked back into the classroom. Arthur took one look at Mr Orme's laptop on the floor and his face lit up like it was Christmas. It was the stuff his dreams were made of.

"39, 56," Ralphy explained.

Bea checked through the playground windows. It seemed that Finley had dropped the chip outside, because the man was scouring the sandpit for his treasure. Inside, Finlay was dissembling Rosie the robot with incredible efficiency and Orme's tools.

Miss Giggle was nursing Holly with a cold compress on her eye.

Arthur placed the laptop on the table. "Password?" he asked.

"39, 56," said Ralphy.

"Well if anyone has clocked a number, it's you," said Arthur. "No," said Arthur, "not it."

Ralphy thought for a second. "42, 59," he said.

"I hope you're not plucking these out of that loose brain of yours," said Arthur arrogantly.

Ralphy smiled.

"Wow, we're in," said Arthur. "He's set his password to update by three every day, eh? And it must've just updated, and you clocked that, Ralphy. Impressive."

Ralphy humbly looked at the computer. The manufacturing logo flashed up on the screen. Bea recognised it. It was the three white stars circling the points of a triangle. Under it was: "Astrostar Innovations".

"Okay, Mr Orme, let's see what you're up to," Arthur said. "You realise, Ralphy, that robot is a ruse, don't you?" Ralphy looked bewildered. "Astrostar Innovations is a multi-billion-dollar, high-tech company; it's not interested in a bunch of autistic kids playing with a crappy robot."

*Three white stars were on the observation plane in Vietnam, where Astrostar made their reputation and money. Arthur's right: they aren't interested in autistic kids and robots.*

Arthur speedily flicked through the contents of the laptop and accessed their school's file.

Miss Cotton and a caretaker held the captive Harvey firmly under the armpits with his legs sky-walking and carried him into the classroom, while Harvey raged. "Off that computer. Make good choices, Arthur!" said Miss Cotton firmly as she walked by.

"I'm gonna need a distraction," said Arthur to Finley, without taking his eyes off the computer.

*More distraction,* thought Bea. *Like what?* Finley was reluctant to leave his incomplete task, so he scooped up what he could of Rosie the robot's pieces and headed for the playground door just as Orme entered. Orme snatched Finley's arm, "Oye!" he shouted angrily.

This was too much aggression for Boundless, who forgot his sore leg, put his head down and rammed Orme. Miss Cotton let go of Harvey, to tackle Orme. Orme didn't know what knocked him down, but Harvey ran light-footedly over the top of him. Finley gathered up pieces of the robot and scattered them like seeds in the wind over the playground fence. Orme followed Finley, howling in despair, and Miss Cotton stood by the door to keep an eye on the intruder. Pip discovered a few robot pieces in the playground. He found a perfect, smooth piece of robot to skim with, rubbed his hands backwards and forwards with delight over the object and wandered off with it.

Miss Cotton noted Arthur was still tapping away at Orme's laptop in the corner. She decided to ignore his IT ban and question him after Orme had left.

Ralphy was absorbed in the multiplication square on the wall.

"Ralphy," Bea shouted, dragging him back to the computer.

Arthur picked up his fidget toy and drawled in an American accent, used to show his superiority over mere tech peasantry. "The toy robot is a guise. Orme's interested in you dumb-butts. Don't ask me why," Arthur said.

Bea recognised the insulting sarcasm. *I'm not sure why people are able to speak when they've nothing kind to say.*

"Here's you, Ralphy." A summary appeared and Arthur read it: "Passive, unpresent, self-harming, obsessed by numbers, semi-verbal. Headbutted the robot." Ralphy smiled. "Suitability factor 15 per cent."

"15," said Ralphy, pleased with the number.

"It seems they are looking for a particular type of non-verbal idiot," Arthur drawled. "Oh, Morgan's here, must've found it!"

*Arthur doesn't think he's clever really*, Bea calculated, *or he wouldn't bother to insult us.*

"Morgan, uncompassionate, rage, easily distracted, unfocused, average intelligence. Suitability factor 72 per cent."

"Wow, they prefer Morgan. They're looking for a psycho," Arthur surmised.

Ralphy pointed to Bea's name and looked at Bea. Her heart was pounding. She was beginning to suspect terrible things. What had Eternal said about her? She was a psychopath waiting to happen. She was feeling sick and dizzy.

"Stay focused," she said to herself.

"Bea," said Arthur. "Uncompassionate, focused, rage and aggression, intelligent." Arthur paused, "Really?"

Ralphy nodded.

"Rebellious and demand avoidant, semi-verbal. Suitability factor 98 per cent. Yep, she's the psycho they're after!" said Arthur in a matter-of-fact tone.

"Wow, and guess what? Both of them were in an accident with the minibus and ended up in hospital." Arthur continued, "Coincidence? I don't think so."

Ralphy began to hyperventilate.

Arthur was obliviously continuing his deductions, "So, either they want to kill the psychos or use them in some big experiment, and take their brains apart, because they can't talk. Good news is they don't want you, Ralphy."

Ralphy was kneeling down hitting his head on the floor, overloaded by the information and the gravity of the situation. Arthur sighed, "Like that helps, Ralphy!"

Bea teetered on the edge of the abyss. *They want to take my brains out!* Then she remembered the men snatching her classmates. *They want to take everyone's brains out! Breathe Bea, Breathe! We're in trouble! Big trouble: Morgan is in the hospital bed, my body has a shaved head, men will be marching down the corridor to pull Pip from Miss Cotton's arms. Hold it together, Bea. Calm focus. Astrostar Innovations caused the accident that put Morgan and myself in hospital, and my mum's agreed to a procedure to take my brain out, because I'm the psycho they're looking for. 98 per cent psycho! Exposed! Shamed!*

*No one understands! I'm imprisoned! I've bars on my mouth! I can't speak anything I need to say! I rage at everyone! No one understands! Everything burns me up with irritation! Everything is always too much! I'm overwhelmed constantly! They're not anxious every day that their mum will leave her and never return, because they're unlovable!*

*Everyone knows I'm out of control and they all smile that 'we don't really like you' smile. They've always known, always looked at me, like I was born violent. I see them swerve to avoid me, avoid my mum and isolate us. I'm an electric fence to be avoided. Even my dad left because of me! All I can cause is pain! And I can't change myself! I'm a lost cause! An unlovable psycho!*

Her emotions engulfed her. She was burning in her tortured thoughts. Crippled in soul-ache, jaded with the emotional pain and shame. She went down to the ground in a stream of violence, knocking Arthur off his chair. She beat every part of her body with self-loathing against the cold, hard floor. Miss Cotton couldn't see Bea to take her to the padded room to calm down, or to put some blankets around her, to hold her or rock her. She rolled in the private, unseeable agony of unloveliness.

Boundless lay down gently next to her to soak up some of her pain. She grabbed his coat, but nothing helped the searing, emotional agony draining her life force, pulling her to pieces. There was nowhere for her emotions to go but her body. With a final crack of the head, she knocked herself out and a dark peace washed over her.

Ralphy burst into tears in anguish. Miss Cotton put a cushion under Ralphy's head as he headbutted the floor. She snatched the laptop from Arthur, pushed it into Mr Orme's chest and escorted the offensive man back to reception. On the way, she explained carefully that if he darkened her door again, he would be arrested for manhandling Finley.

Harvey stared at the cupboard for a drink and biscuit, but Miss Giggle was busy comforting Ralphy, so he retreated to an empty gaze.

Miss Giggle put number songs on the whiteboard and Ralphy calmed as he and Pip absorbed themselves in the order and simplicity and safe feelings of counting in sevens, zoning out into the sanctuary of Number Land.

Finley had managed to hold on to a few robot parts and a screwdriver and sat seriously at a table trying to make "a thing".

Holly sat down to write a letter to Miss Cotton to tell her that she did not like the robot man.

Miss Cotton returned to an orderly classroom, and after quizzing Arthur, who could tell her nothing, she sent him back to Miss Thompson's classroom. She sat on her desk as the children calmed to serenity and watched Finley. She thought, *the morning hasn't been a complete waste; Finley's engineering skills have definitely improved.*

# 10

# Grandma's

Bea was looking up at an incredibly blue sky – so blue it tasted of blueberries with a hint of mint. She felt coolness all around, nourishing her, like water. She heard the splash from her hand, *Oh, it is water!* A nose nuzzled her and as she reached towards it, she looked straight into the eyes of a humongous pink and brown dinosaur. She was shocked.

"You weren't who I was expecting," she cried.

"Why not?" asked the dinosaur.

"She thought you were a sheep," Boundless explained, water dripping from his mouth.

"Am I?" the dinosaur asked.

"Nope, I am," Boundless explained, patiently.

"You're talking," said Bea to Boundless.

"Yes," said the dinosaur. "I use this," and it stuck out its tongue.

*I'm in the Kingdom.* She was delighted as she sat up to stroke the large, inquisitive nose. It sneezed.

"Did you do that?" the dinosaur asked her.

"No, you did it," Bea laughed.

"Did I?" said the dinosaur, surprised.

Boundless sighed, and took another drink.

Everything seemed delicious: the sky, the clouds, the water. She was released into the freedom and lightness of being like a bird taking flight, her senses sharp and her head clear, calm and hopeful. She was lusciously alive. Looking around her, she saw that she was sitting in the hugest, clearest, bluest puddle she could ever imagine. Right in front of her Ralphy was laughing with a smaller dinosaur, as if they were sharing a joke. She stood up dripping with pleasure, as each drop left her clothes. Harvey was lying on his back, outstretched in the shallow pond, flicking the water around him with a crazily happy face, completely joyful.

Ralphy's green and yellow dinosaur did a dump.

"Oh, you pooed," said Ralphy.

Bea nearly fell backwards; she was so shocked at hearing Ralphy say something that wasn't numbers.

"What did you call it?" asked the larger dinosaur to Ralphy.

"A poo," said Ralphy.

"Did I do that?" said the smaller dinosaur.

"Apoo?" said the larger dinosaur, laughing.

Ralphy was splitting himself laughing. "A poo!" repeated Ralphy.

"Apoo? Was it me?" asked the little dinosaur.

Ralphy and the big dinosaur were rolling around in the water laughing, as the little dinosaur kept examining his poo and saying, "Did I do that? Really? Was it me?"

Boundless nuzzled Bea's hand. She looked down.

He shook his head. "That's why they're extinct," he sighed. "I've a few sheep to see. I'll catch you later?"

Bea was still drinking in the puddled dinosaurs, Ralphy talking, Harvey's happiness, the spacious peace of the place and her own joy at being there. Nothing was demanded of her and she didn't feel the need for any reassurance.

"Okay," she said to Boundless, who had regained his supersonic speed and already disappeared.

Bea watched Harvey flicking the water happily at himself. "Hey, do you come here all the while?"

Harvey turned and grinned at her. "Course, wouldn't you?" he asked, as he turned onto his stomach to do a pretend swim. She'd never heard Harvey speak, and his voice was full of intonation and humour.

Pip appeared in the water, holding a colourful paper boat in his hand, with numbers on it.

"Look at its trajectory," squealed Pip in anticipation as he blew it and the boat sailed into the sky on its own pre-planned course. Pip eagerly followed it.

"Hey, this is where you go when you're spaced out at school!"

"It's just a different kind of school," said Ralphy, standing behind her.

"Why don't I go to this school?" asked Bea, feeling a jealous cloud of anxiety appear on the horizon.

"Want to go and see Grandma?" Ralphy asked.

Bea wanted to hold on to the feeling of unfairness, but it had already evaporated. *Who's Grandma?* Expressions of Grandma surrounded Bea, with the smell of cookies baking, a whisper of crisp cotton and hearty laughter, she felt fingers pressed into squidgy icing and tasted butterscotch and marshmallows. *Oh yes, I want to be there!*

Ralphy ran through the puddle, Bea followed. They didn't run for long. There was no sense of effort, but after a brief blur of blue and brown, they were in a side passage of a sunny town and had slowed down to a walk.

On the left-hand side of the alleyway, cafes jostled with tables and chairs arranged outside and people chatting over drinks and food. On the right-hand side, a wicker fence finished at eye height with orange trees fruitfully hanging over. The pavement beyond the fence was raised so she could just see people's feet walking by. A series of decorative wooden arches curved over the passageway. Everything was made with incredible care and attention to detail, as if there was more than enough time to show how much the crafter loved their job.

Each cafe was unique. One smelt of berries and bananas and the chat was ripe and fruity and bubbly. Another was rich and earthy with deep, woody conversation, wholesome scones and homemade soup. Another was delicate and the conversation frothed with bubble tea and smelt of mint and apples.

A tall slim woman looked up from her bubble tea. She was leaning on a counter, next to a friend, enthusiastically discussing her experience of life. She seemed to recognise Bea, as she caught her eye. Bea was caught off guard, because the woman acknowledged her being there, as if Bea's existence mattered, as if she was worth something just because of who she was. Bea wasn't used to being seen in such an intimate and yet totally generous way and was taken aback. Before she'd had time to work out how she might know the woman, a man in a cafe smelling of fresh, homegrown tomatoes and chillis and the heat of heartfelt conversation waved at her. *I don't know how I know you, but it's like you have always seen me and you just wanted me to know that.* The chatter from the cafe warmed her skin, and she just wanted to indulge herself in it.

"Where's my cat?" said Ralphy and, as if summoned by the need, a small, slinky black cat appeared on one of the arches. It arched its back and took a leap into Ralphy's arms. "Ah, there you are." Ralphy sighed contentment and the cat purred.

Above the sounds of the chatter, Bea heard birds chirping, the humming of bees in the hanging baskets of flowers, the flip of sandals. What was missing? There were no cars. No clanking of deliveries, drilling of roadworks and no electric hiss from pylons. No phones! She looked around again – no phones, and everyone was chatting happily away as if on some amazing holiday.

She smelt the coffee as if it was the first waft of a crushed bean ground in a pestle and mortar and sifted through fine gauze. The coffee house conversation was creamy with compassion and rich with earnestness. The burnt-sugar topping of truth filtered through the woven wicker chairs and plump yellow cushions. Sunflowers listened attentively around the sides of the cafe. A young Asian man paused his coffee cup and looked directly up at her. He smiled deeply of recognition and memory. She reverberated with connection; in his eyes she saw the old man from Vietnam. She paused to smile back, knowing they had both cared.

Boundless slowed down to a walk and finally stopped on the bank of the lake. He contemplated his reflection for a moment and laughed. The water rippled out. His eyes scanned the lake, where a huge mountain was reflected in it. The lake was so still, the mountain was exposed in all its detail and colour. His eyes drifted up to focus on the true mountain above the reflection. Together, they created a sense of wholeness and unity, as if it took both the mountain and its reflection to create the fullness of itself. Boundless began the climb to the top of the mountain.

The smell of the bakery was overwhelmingly good. Ralphy and Bea stopped to breathe it in. It was bread in the oven, French almond croissants, cheese scones and cake mixed with the buttery, sugary goodness that said you would never feel hungry again and a slight after-smell of tangy blackcurrant jam. Ralphy pushed open the door to Grandma's bakery. A bell rang. 'Welcome,' it sang.

The cafe counter was dark wood and long. The whole counter was adorned in large, decorated cakes filled with cream, marzipan, icing and meringue that puffed up in mountainous peaks a foot high. Nothing was small, simple or undecorated. The rainbow cake sparkled with rainbow glitter and coloured, jellied fruit. The icing fruit cake had a fountain of yellow flowers falling through the layers. The strawberry tart was piled so high with strawberries that the one on top rocked gently, threatening to fall off into a tray of profiteroles competing for height. The cheesecakes were layered and wider than any pizza she had ever seen. Right next to Bea stood a huge, proud coffee cake with generous fresh coffee cream piled high and sprinkled with chocolate quills and crumbled nuts.

The next minute, Ralphy's cat was trying to jump for the cream when, all of a sudden, it was all over Bea's chin and neck, hair, on her pyjama top and bottoms and in Ralphy's face. The woman next to them was laughing as if fit to burst and shouting, "It was me. I did it. Ha ha ha!" She demonstrated her batting of the cream, "Puff!"

This was Grandma! The essence of comfort, the cuddle you are missing, the cake you need and the shoulder you know is there. Ralphy was licking the cream and laughing, and the black cat was standing on Bea's shoulder licking cream off Bea's neck. Bea hesitated. *In an old existence I might have raged that I was covered in cream and had fatty spots all over my clothes. But how sad it would be to miss the opportunity to laugh*. Before she knew it, her head threw back unexpectedly and a choked-up laugh came out of her mouth, as if for the first time, until she roared with laughter and felt an upswelling of joy. She couldn't resist it. She scooped up a dollop of cream and threw it at Grandma, who was laughing at the cream in her hair as she brought her arms around Bea and said, "Welcome home Bea. Oh, I have missed you, honey."

The coffee cake rearranged itself, and added chocolate curls and small golden stars. "Don't you just love it when the head chef adds the finishing touches," she said, admiring the cake.

"Bea, sugar, you have post in the corner, when you're ready," Grandma indicated, smiling.

Ralphy went to find a table and Bea went behind the counter to search for the post. There it was: a small brown envelope with "wage slip for Beattie" written neatly by someone who loved writing, and a letter in a white envelope that said "BeA", with a smiley, slightly lopsided face on it. She turned to spot the author in the cafe guests. The guests hummed with warm, baked love, topped with drizzles of affection and dollops of attachment. The author wasn't there.

A young, golden woman with a soft-baked heart and melting embrace was serving Denzil. "Oh no, Denzil, this is our treat today, just for you, lovely one." Denzil beamed at the specialness of receiving such a gift. "Next time," she said, "but do take one of these for the journey?"

"Oh no," said Denzil, "I'm so full."

The next customer, came to pay. "I tell you what, sweetheart," said soft-bake. "It's on the house for you today, Loren. I've never seen anyone enjoy that mandarin meringue like you." And so it went on. Every customer so special, so important, so loved.

When Bea joined Ralphy, Grandma had just brought over two milkshakes with ice cream on top and a slice of blackcurrant gateau and rainbow cake and three gingerbread biscuits. "You let me know when you're ready for more," said Grandma in a warm, encouraging tone. "Don't you worry, it's on the house for you two today. I'm so thrilled you're here." She took Bea's hand and connected with her eyes, "Ah Bea, you are the secret ingredient in my family recipe, the spice that warms my soul. You're the nutmeg that makes the egg flan taste divine. Only you can bring that smell and taste to this banquet. How satisfying you are." She gave her another hug. Bea felt a unique value she had never known. She was of worth.

Boundless arrived at the top of the mountain, puffing from the extra weight he was carrying. He walked into the circle of stone seats carved into the mountain peak. He shook off his wool coat with the heavy, damp mist and snowflakes attached and sat down on one of the seats clasping his hands together. He smelt the fresh, crisp air of the mountain breeze. His eyes rested on the breathtaking views and vast perspective that could only be seen from that vantage point. His ears listened to the wise thoughts and heartfelt words that drifted from the other occupants of the mountain seats and out with the breeze. "Will you return with her?" one asked. "Yes," he replied. "You have Boundless hope," a wise voice said. "Boundless heart," said another. "Boundless patience," said a third.

The cakes were enormous. "Let's share," said Ralphy. Bea had never, in her whole, short life, shared anything off her plate. This was autistic etiquette: "Mine is mine alone." But there, at Grandma's, she couldn't think of anything more wonderful than to share her food with Ralphy.

"I love you, Ralphy," she said, surprised that those words had just popped themselves randomly out of her head, into her mouth and into the delicious atmosphere. "I know," said Ralphy, giving her one of his heart-searching stares. "I love cake," he said.

It was the best moment ever. The best tea party. It was a time of unknown friendship and heartfelt kindness and she felt truly happy. She fitted like a twig on a tree. She was part of the banquet of life.

"This place is not serious," she said. "It's heaven?"

"It's home," said Ralphy.

She looked at her letters. She knew that other things called. She sensed them closing in. "I better open them," she sighed. The wage slip read:

"Bea:

| 1 | curly whirly slide, |
| 1 | set of circular steps, |
| 1 | sea shell bed." |

"I got paid," she said to Ralphy. Ralphy still had a straw in his mouth as he looked over her shoulder at the wage slip, and the straw was dripping milkshake. The milkshake dripped onto the wage slip. An unusual thought appeared: *How lovely, milky splodges on the paper.*

"That is not my thought," said Bea, laughing. She picked up her straw and blew some milkshake gently up into the air and watched it settle on the table. Ralphy laughed and followed suit.

"That's for your home," said Ralphy. "A slide is so cool."

"Yeah," said Bea, "it's going out of my bedroom window."

"Oh, I forgot," said Ralphy. "These are for you." He took a screwed-up piece of paper out of his pocket, the sort he liked to chew on, and opened it up. He picked up a seed and placed it in Bea's hands, counting as he did it. "One, two, three." That was it – three little seeds as small as grains of rice.

"Thanks," she said. "I'll plant them on the end of my slide." She grinned and Ralphy beamed. She placed them in her pay packet and carefully popped it in her pocket.

She felt a woolly nuzzle underneath the table – Boundless had snuck into the cafe and smelt something delicious on the table. *Ah, that's who the biscuits were for.* She smiled and passed him one under the table and heard him crunching. She smiled and passed another.

"What's in the letter?" asked Ralphy.

She opened the envelope. It read:

"DeAr MiSs CotTon,

I Do Not LiKe THe RoBot Man. He FriTens Pip. WheRe Is Morgan and BeA? Wen Are TheY BaCk in ScHool. I don't Like ChaiNg. I Like PizZa.

I LoVe You

HolLy X"

It flooded back to her: Orme, from Astrostar Innovations; Arthur and the laptop, the men dragging off her classmates. She had to get back to save her body and find Morgan too.

Bea turned to Ralphy, "I've got to go back." But Ralphy had already disappeared. She reached for Boundless's ear and lurched forward.

# 11

## Morgan

Bea and Boundless slid down the mattresses and scrambled off as quickly as possible. Boundless swung round to bleat-growl at the encroaching bedding, while Bea leapt over to the cleaner's table to inspect the state of her body. The chairs were empty, the ashtray full. The cleaner's had tidied away her body. *Why would they do that? I hate people moving my things! Especially something that important!*

She sat on a recently wiped chair and tried to breathe deeply, "I'm nutmeg in an egg flan. I'm an essential ingredient. I am worthwhile. I'm recognised in the kingdom and I have a slide and a seashell bed waiting for me. I'm expected home."

The sincerity of the words warmed her, so she repeated them. Boundless turned to observe her.

"You didn't need to come back here. That's your home. You've got sheep family; you can't even talk here. Why would you leave the Kingdom for me? I should've told you to stay, but I was thinking of me. Sorry." She gave him a hug and felt an unusual emotion: *grateful. I feel grateful.* "Thank you, Boundless. I really need you."

"I don't know where to start? I need to find my body. Maybe they took it back upstairs to the ward? Yes, I think so. The ward number is on the wrist tag. I need to find Morgan. I need to get past the mattresses. I feel overwhelmed already!"

Boundless listened, then looked at the biscuit wrapper.

"That's not the answer this time," she said. "We have to think, think wider. We have to understand the ... the context."

*Wow, where has that word come from? I definitely haven't heard it before, but I know what it means!*

Bea stood up to pace, because that worked last time. *I'm learning what works for me and implementing it.*

"The context," she said to Boundless. "Vietnam. President Kennedy didn't want a war and neither did the Vietnamese leader, Ngo Dinh Diem."

She paused, "I probably didn't pronounce that right, but I'm gobsmacked I remembered him."

She continued, "So this world order assassinated them because it wanted a war. The world order is paid by these companies. No, that's not right – the world order existed before these companies, it's bigger than these companies, they're just a cog in the machine. So, the world order replaces the new President of the USA, with ...". Bea visualised the old TV. "President Lyndon Johnson, their puppet president, so that they can have a war. Why?"

Boundless was eating the biscuit wrapper.

"So they can decrease the population by killing off GIs? So they can get the USA out of an economic slump? And give these companies war-related contracts?"

*How do I know what economic slump is? How do I know about war-related contracts?*

"What is behind this group of financial tycoons? Why are they killing off world leader's everywhere and replacing them, just to increase profit?"

Boundless was tired of being the audience and had joined in the pacing.

"Turn around that way, Boundless," Bea directed. They paced the other way.

"The world order isn't a few people in a dingy room wringing their hands and plotting the downfall of the next president. Their interventions cover centuries. There must be a driving force that unites them – an aim, an idea. What did President Kennedy say? 'An idea lives on'. They want to achieve something – out of war. Something more than money."

*I'm sure Eternal's listening and smirking, but I have to tie it all together to create a bigger picture.*

"What did Churchill say? 'World order or world anarchy.' So, they are frightened of rebellion? Of riots and protests and placards? They didn't expect the peace protests, 'make love, not war'. They killed Kennedy, but they couldn't kill the idea, of peace. Are they frightened of love? Well I guess it is scary."

Bea stopped. Boundless walked into the back of her legs. She turned to talk to him, "We're going down a rabbit hole and I'm not sure we've got the map."

Boundless gazed up at her with sheepish eyes. "Why did you come back? Was it for me? Are you involved with this?"

*How could he be? He's a sheep, a talking sheep, but he only talks in the Kingdom. If he was involved, he'd come as something powerful, like a dragon.*

"Nothing is certain," she said to the sheep. "But, I don't think so, sorry." Bea was conscious that she didn't normally apologise, unless it was a reluctant, grumpy "Sorry!" forced out by an insistent adult and guilt-ridden circumstances.

"Okay," said Bea, talking directly to Boundless. "Why is Astrostar Innovations that made Quiet Hawk stealth surveillance now after a bunch of autistic kids that have meltdowns and can't talk? Do they want us to be spies? Do you think we'd make good spies? We're overwhelmed by everything! We stick out like pink, fluorescent bananas?" *That was a very creative description! And to top it off, I'm identifying my use of imaginative language!*

"Does problem-solving get easier? I'm still missing pieces of the jigsaw! The only person who has answers is Eternal, and how is he connected to this? I wish you could speak, you big daft sheep. I really need help," Bea moaned.

"I see you're talking to the sheep now," said Eternal, entering through the wall, to the sound of his name, wearing his dark suit and black glasses.

"He's the only one who makes any sense," answered Bea, hearing a different intonation in her voice.

"That's a tone of cynicism I hear," said Eternal, taking his glasses off. "Getting world-weary?"

"Of some things," muttered Bea.

"Sarcasm. You must've learnt something at school?"

"Yes," said Bea, trying to redirect her focus from her recent blackout. "Astrostar Innovations made surveillance planes in Vietnam. They're a multi-million, big-tech company now. They caused the minibus accident. Morgan's in hospital somewhere. I need to rescue him, and my body, before they perform an operation that may do something to my beautiful brain – save the world and get home for tea."

"I didn't eat the medical notes," said Eternal, looking at the sheep. "Else you'd know exactly what they were doing and why."

It sowed a seed of doubt. Bea scrutinised Boundless. He snuffled closer.

"You sounded like you knew what the operation was for?" stated Bea.

"You wanted to go on this journey by yourself, without my interference. Have you changed your mind? I've always been trying to help you, Bea," said Eternal conceitedly.

"Have you?" Bea asked.

"Of course; I'm your life-teacher. There are two universal rules left to break."

*I'm reluctant to break another rule, Eternal's game feels rigged, with only one possible outcome: Eternal wins. What does he win? He said I could decide if it was a good destiny before I break rule nine. So, I can refuse to break rule nine. But, the surgeons could be operating. I need to get moving now. What universal rule did I witness in the Kingdom?*

"We are all connected."

Eternal was surprised and pleased: "Everything is connected. Well done, Bea! Rule eight. One rule to complete."

A magnetic pull was tingling through her feet and up to her backbone. She grabbed Boundless' ear, as Eternal disappeared.

"He looks ecstatic! One rule to go!" Bea cried to Boundless as the drag that began in the centre of her spine hauled her swiftly over the mattresses and up the stairs backwards, with Boundless bumping up the stairs on his bottom, attached to Bea by the ear.

"I feel like I'm on a fishing line," Bea shouted as she bashed open the doors, whacking her body on the swing and Boundless catching the rebound. It heaved her down the corridor, bumping the odd nurse, doctor and evening cleaner out of the way. It clattered its way through double doors with Boundless bleating, as he was swung from side to side by his two ears.

Bea had been trying to work out whether it was better to hold on to Boundless or let go. She let go and he flew down the corridor, bowling the cleaner over. She smashed through double doors stating they had reached Children's Intensive Care. *I'm going back to my body*!

She collided into a nurse holding a coffee. It went all over her uniform. The nurse was bending down to wipe herself as Boundless skidded on the spilt coffee and skittled the same nurse again. Bea banged through a ward door and the connection plonked her on the bed. Boundless skidded through the door and crashed into the bedpost. He rattled his ears and shook the coffee off his coat.

Bea breathed heavily and stared at the woman asleep in a chair by her bed. *They swopped my mum!* She inspected the body in the bed – it was Morgan sleeping in his Batman pyjamas.

It was a smaller, two-bed ward, similar to Bea's, but with plastic curtains dividing the two patients. They were the same type of grubby green and yellow walls, and an old-fashioned monitor. She looked out of the window at the night sky and heard the nurse tiptoeing down the corridor with her new coffee.

Bea snatched Morgan's notes, giving Boundless a glare, and sat cross-legged on the bed. Morgan's head was bandaged but apart from that he seemed undamaged. He looked more peaceful than she'd ever known him. *This is why my mum watches me sleep – only time I'm angelic.*

"Morgan!" she shout-whispered. "Morgan, it's Bea. Wake up, we've got to talk!" Morgan didn't move. *In fact, he looks just like my body, except I assaulted mine down the stairs.*

Morgan clutched her wrist. "I thought you were asleep," she said to him, too loudly, he didn't open his eyes and his arm relaxed while he held her. "It's me, Bea. Let go," she whispered. He didn't.

Morgan and Bea had not got on, because Bea enjoyed winding Morgan up. She used to watch to see what game he wanted and take it first, wait until he wriggled for the loo and get in there first. Miss Cotton said they were too alike, but she knew she was smarter.

"Well, the monitor says you're alive and your notes say you're in an induced coma?" Bea whispered to him. *That's not a coincidence, that we're both in comas. That means my coma's induced too! Why would the hospital choose to put kids in comas? Unless they've an agreement with Astrostar Innovations, to take our brains out!*

She peered under the bandage at a neat 4 cm scar. *It's in the same location as my shaved hair. If he's in a coma, maybe he's around here somewhere? Surely, I'd see him.* Bea flicked the curtain up on the next cubicle with her toes, to see a battered and bruised teenage boy watching the late-night news, while scrolling on his phone.

"Get off, Morgan!" she whispered, trying to remove Morgan's offending hand, still gripping her wrist. She followed the drip tube to a bag with a Chemoxic logo on it. It was the same manufacturer that had made the napalm cannisters.

"They're feeding you liquid napalm!" she cried, horrified. She checked the tag on the bottom of the bag for confirmation, but the drug wasn't napalm. According to his medical notes, it was for 'mild pain relief'. *He doesn't look like he's in pain.*

She flicked past the medical terms in Morgan's notes to the following page. "Operation successful. But this is three weeks ago? The kids in school are just making us a card? How can it be three weeks ago?" *How can I have lost three weeks? I was at school, ate cake, came back to the hospital. I didn't spend three weeks at Grandma's. Eternal would've said something.*

"How come you're still in a coma? If the operation was successful?" she muttered to Morgan "I don't get it."

She scoured the notes. Morgan had been on a programme of treatment, but at stage three, there had been a violent reaction to the drugs, and the programme had been terminated.

*Well, I'm not taking drugs, and I'm not surprised Morgan wouldn't take them. He wouldn't take a sweetie if you offered it to him. Of course, if you're in a coma, and the drugs are intravenous, how can you refuse.*

Bea read the last page: "Adverse brain damage, short-term life expectancy, two months, terminal." She read it again.

*Morgan's going to die? Astrostar Innovations crashed the bus on purpose. The hospital put him in a coma, gave him drugs his body rejected and now he's going to die! They've murdered him! Everything is connected!*

Morgan's other hand was around her waist.

"Get off, Morgan," said Bea. "I've got to get back to my own body; they're going to murder me too! I can't help you! I'll thump you! You know I will, even if you're dying! If you don't let go!"

She could feel Morgan's stomach against her back, his arm was wrapped around her waist. She couldn't twist herself around to whack him.

"Get off," she shouted, wriggling and twisting. *What if three weeks have passed and they've already operated on me?*

"Get off me, I'm being murdered somewhere! I need my own body! Morgan! Get off! You've got your own consciousness; you don't need mine! We are not connecting this way!"

She was lying down on top of him, with her head and neck desperately fighting to stay upright. *This is all going horribly wrong. I'm going to end up in Morgan's head. Even if I find mine, how will I get out of Morgan's body? I bet Eternal's laughing himself stupid! That smug, hypocritical, two-faced creep. He knows I've*

*only one rule left to get myself out of this, now I'll have to use it!*
*Unless, Morgan doesn't wake up and I die in his body in a coma!*

She reached out, and Boundless nuzzled into her palm. *I can't fight it. It's too powerful! Help me, Boundless!* The pillow smelt damp and musty. She was exhausted by stress, overwhelmed by panic. *If I could just relax and let go for a moment, I could think.* Bea relaxed into the mattress.

"The mattress! Oh no!" she whimpered as she let go of her last willpower.

# 12

# The gloom

Bea sank below the surface. Her energy spent, with no solution, she drifted into the deepness of a muffled quiet and was still. The mattresses settled down, sighing with contentment at their new addition. She was embedded in a collective gloom. There was nothing to get up for, ever. She could drift, she could rest.

Bea's head fuzzed over and for a while she forgot everything. She knew there were universal rules, but they slipped out of her head before she could form them, so she submerged herself in an old feeling she couldn't identify.

Memories sifted by. Eventually, a memory arrived as a visual replay, except she was a third party watching the event from a distance.

She could see herself, aged 11, standing in the kitchen, spreadeagled in the doorway, refusing to let her mum through to the living room. Her mum was leaning against the kitchen radiator, her hand rubbed her eyes and spread down her face to her chin in an attempt to wipe the tension off.

"I don't know what to do with you, Bea." Her mum was pleading, "You're exhausting me. What do you want? I can't make it better."

"You're a stink-bomb, sucker!" she'd screamed at her mother, over a stain on her school shirt, now slopped on the draining board covered in detergent.

"I can't manage another one of your moods," she entreated. "I've been at work all day. Please stop it! It's just a stain. I can't get it off!" She looked exhausted.

"You, you, you," Bea was stamping and raging.

"I didn't do it!" Her mum was getting annoyed. "You did it! You did it at school!"

"You! You!" said Bea, hitting her with fury. Her mum slipped through the door and ran for the bathroom with Bea running behind her. "You, you, bad mother!" she screamed.

The bathroom door clicked as it locked. Bea slammed into it, bashing the door with her fists.

Through the door her mum was breathing deeply and trying to gulp back sobs. Bea launched herself at the door, before sliding down it and periodically whacking her head backwards into her Mum's only exit.

Her mum was on the phone, her voice echoing bathroom loneliness. "I'm so alone, Marion. I don't know what to do any more. No one can put up with this!"

Bea slammed the back of her head into the door. "You, bad mother," she growled. "You. It really hurt and then some!"

Bea sat on the floor and waited. She knew her mum would have to come out, and apologise for the shirt. She had felt justice that her mum was suffering, because she hadn't sorted the shirt out and she should have. Bea wasn't asking for a lot! The stain had to be removed. Now, her mum knew her pain. She would try harder and remove the stain. Bea didn't think about what if the stain couldn't be removed. That would mean the shirt would be lost and Bea couldn't manage the thought of such a horrendous loss. Loss was a dreadful feeling. It reminded her of other losses. Loss of her favourite shoes when they wouldn't fit, loss of her plastic whale, loss of her voice.

Now her mum was alone and frightened and despairing, because Bea was alone with her pain.

Bea reflected: *I am that person. That's how I behaved, if something wasn't right. I caused that pain, to my mum. I did it regularly. I hurt people and I didn't care, as long as they felt my pain and as long as I got what I needed.*

Black claws gripped the insides of her stomach and twisted the guilt. As she recaptured the scene, they ripped into her lungs and pierced her throat until she was trembling with utter remorse. Tears gushed out as she rocked herself, sobbing and crying for who she was and what she had done. Her heart stung, her sides ached and still the tears poured out. *I can't take it back. I did it. I can't change anything. I'm so, so lost.*

She drifted, exhausted. She felt the mattresses protect her from a world she couldn't participate in and didn't understand. She would never fit into or be able to communicate with it. A world that grated on every nerve until the force of it found its freedom in hurting someone else. *Here, I'm safe. Here, others are safe. There's no reason to get up.*

Memories flooded in again, distanced by time and external perspective, one after the other, showing cold, ugly truth and evoking bitter remorse.

She watched herself standing in a supermarket aisle holding on to at least seven packets of sweets and chocolates. She was 12.

Her mum was carrying Bea's schoolbag on her back. She looked up from the biscuit selection and smiled, "There's too many there, Bea. Put some back, please. Choose three."

"No. No way. No," Bea had growled, threatening the supermarket meltdown that everyone stared at. The one where she told the whole shop loudly that her mum was a bad mother. She had placed the threat as if it was a box of fireworks and she held the match. She rattled the packets of sweets to gauge her mum's reaction.

"You'll get fat eating all of that," Mum cajoled, playing for time.

"No way. No." Bea stamped her foot, aware that the presence of fireworks tipped everything in her favour.

Her mum looked around the busy aisle. People had already stopped shopping to inspect the shouting and assess the risk. "Put them in the trolley." Her mum sounded depressed and her shoulders sagged with powerlessness.

Bea felt the control, smiled and placed them all in the trolley.

Her mum walked to the end of the aisle with Bea and took the extra tasty sausages and a chocolate treat she had in mind for herself out of the trolley and put them back on the fruit juice shelf. Mum's face had dropped to hopelessness and it annoyed Bea. Bea threw a packet of the sweets across the aisle and stamped on them.

Her mum looked horrified. "It's okay, I don't mind. Have them," she was lying.

Bea sighed loudly and turned away to give her the silent treatment, and walked out of the store. Her mum had no choice but to follow; the shopping trip was over!

*I never realised what it cost Mum. The endless embarrassment, the drama over everything. The constant tension that I might kick off, the pain and humiliation of giving in and having to pretend to be happy about it or she'd get the silent treatment too. I was cruel and unkind.*

*I never saw my mum, what she needed, the little things she missed out on, and the big things like holidays and friends. I was selfish and spoilt.*

*But I wasn't a psycho. I wasn't a killer. I was ugly on the inside. Ugly with anger and self-pity and I hated everyone because they couldn't help me. I hated myself more.* Tears gushed out and the mattresses absorbed it all.

The mattresses seemed comfortable and cosy in their gloomy sadness, they too knew a world that was just too painful and sad to be around. An existence of hospital tubes and endlessly waiting for results; pain that made your loved ones irritating and kind nurses grating. The reality of hopes dashed, grieving friends and desperate mothers and fathers. The faded cards wishing you well, and the sadness of people who knew all the wishes in the world wouldn't change the end result. Facing the inevitable, alone, envious of everyone else getting on with the bouncing goodness of living.

She heard a rip, the sniffling of a wet nose breathing fresh life with an impatient snort of a bigger truth. The mattress quivered. She listened as teeth ripped again at the fabric of old life and faded lies. Another rip as renewed hope drifted through the tattered shreds of self-pity. A hoof dug into a coil of self-loathing and teeth grabbed the stains of old behaviour and past mistakes. Tearing, slashing, rip, rip, rip as humble acceptance poured in like sunlight. Boundless's love trashed the mattress as he gripped her pyjamas in his teeth and dragged her out like a newborn.

She helplessly hugged him, tears welling in her eyes. "Thank you," she said with such fresh gratitude. "Thank you, for everything," as again she wept. She hardly had time to wipe her eyes on his wool before Boundless turned to snort at another mattress.

He sniffed the nearest one and, with a rage she had not expected from such a gentle animal, he tore a large section of the cover off. Within a few moments he was pulling the mattress apart. A bruised 6-year-old child lay curled up between the metal springs and the decaying wadding, hiding from a world that had betrayed her and left her helpless. Bea crawled over to the mattress, feeling the isolated sadness of the little girl's rejection. "It's okay, we all feel like that," she consoled, as she pulled out the little one and wrapped her in her arms. She wiped her own tears away and tried to smile. The little girl threw her arms around Bea. "I was so alone. No one came to help me," the little girl gasped, and Bea hugged and rocked her as the child cried. Bea felt the strength and resilience of comforting another, more fragile being.

Boundless watched them comfort each other before targeting another mattress. When Bea heard the material tear, she grabbed the cloth and united in pulling and ripping it apart. It was a young man. Immediately she felt his isolation and deep depression. She hugged him with such empathy and understanding that any embarrassment he'd briefly felt washed away.

"Thank you. I thought I was the only one. I just felt so completely lost," he gasped.

*I'm feeling someone else's feelings. I can empathise. How awesome is that! I care! I actually care about someone else!* And again, Bea burst into tears and hugged the young man.

There was momentum, as the pair joined Boundless to rescue the next child from the pile of depressing, stain-soaked, old cloth mattresses. They were soon hugging and rejoicing, and tears of gratitude wiped away the little embarrassment, as it melted into the joy of being free from their soul-aching misery. They hugged each other with empathy and solace and such kindness that Bea felt driven to find more energy to release the next one. So, it went on, until countless children were rescuing the last few. The fragile honesty of all their new-found freedom, and the relief and hope they expressed, filled Bea with purpose and new intention.

*I will never forget this. We all struggle, but we can all be transformed. No one is beyond hope. No one.*

The mattresses were in a disembowelled heap, as the last five were ripped into. Inside a grubby, stripy, blue and white mattress, was Morgan. He was tangled up in old wire and appeared smaller and more fragile than Bea remembered him. As she pulled him out, he was sobbing like a toddler. She held him in in her arms and rocked him, as Miss Cotton had often done to her. As his sobbing slowed, he asked her, "Did you see yourself, Bea?"

"Yes, I did. I saw a messed-up kid," said Bea. "But, I'm not one any more. I have worth. I'm part of an incredible kingdom, I just didn't believe it until now."

"Mine was dreadful," he said. "I didn't think I could ever face anyone again."

"Silly," said Bea. "You faced me and now we're here together, and we both know each other's pain, don't we, so we're not alone." She smiled.

Morgan hugged her and wept again. She knew this was not the old Morgan: he was humble and gentle and a truer, realer person for his experience. *I guess I am too.*

Bea glanced around her. There were more than seventy children of all ages in the warehouse, empathising with and nurturing each other. Boundless stood by the big warehouse doors sniffing the air wafting underneath them. He stared at her. *It's strange, but my sheep is in charge of its own flock of children.*

"Time to open the doors," she said to Morgan, pulling him to his feet. They pulled up the metal poles holding each door in place and slid the doors back on their runners. The warehouse brightened up and the children stood blinking in the sunshine.

*Freedom. If I'd known what it felt like, I would've searched for it earlier. Freedom from all those crippling, suffocating feelings. I can breathe, I can live, really live.* Bea let out a huge, hearty laugh as she walked into the sunlight.

Boundless led the way into the cobbled street and halted at the first terraced house in the row. In the front of it was a patio with a few unruly plants trying to stay upright in pots. She followed Boundless through the gate and passed a fishing gnome with a sign: "Grandma's house".

"Of course," she said, as if her world now made sense. *The kingdom is always near and Presence must've entered the hospital to liberate us all.*

It was a strange sight: seventy children ambled through the front door of the terraced house and up the narrow stairs. They passed pictures of cottages and white terrier dogs, and into the bedroom on the top of the landing. There was no bed or furniture, just the fluffiest white carpet Bea had ever known. The kids were rolling, giggling, laughing, diving into the woolliness as it cleaned the dust and grime from the mattresses. Bea dropped into a roll in the white carpet as every fleecy fibre removed the last pores of a painful past and promised her a new and brighter future. Spotless and sparkling with excitement, the children galloped into the bluest sky and the greenest grass they'd ever seen as the expansive, pastural landscape filled the back wall.

Bea laughed as she skipped light-heartedly towards her homeland. Her feet hadn't left the carpet when she heard Presence: "Bea, whom shall I send?"

She tried again, desperate to indulge her senses in the pleasure of belonging, and put her feet on the greenest of grass, but she couldn't enter the Kingdom. She turned around. Boundless had her pyjama top in his teeth.

"I need to go," she cried out to Boundless.

Boundless's teeth held firm and his look was serious. He held on as the last of the children went through to the pastured land. Bea relaxed.

"They can't come back, can they? Neither can Morgan." The little girl and young man turned around smiling and waving. Morgan blew her a kiss.

"But it's not my time," she sighed. They danced into the landscape, Bea watched enviously. Boundless looked sheepish as he trotted onto the lush grass. "Not you too, Boundless!"

"You're not alone, Bea. You never were," Boundless said as he turned to face her on the edge of the landscape.

"No, but I'll miss you."

"I'll come back for you. I promise."

"I don't know what I'm doing."

Boundless laughed, "We're not meant to."

The landscape evaporated and the bedroom wall returned.

Bea was alone. She sighed and walked down the stairs of Grandma's house and back into the sunshine toward the hospital.

Bea felt less attached to the fabric of the world. *I have Presence in me. I can feel it. I know a truth I can never unknow, not without being a lie to myself, and I haven't been through all this to become a lie. The truth is alive. I'm going to grow in it. I'm part of something wonderful – I belong to the kingdom.*

"I may not know what I'm doing," said Bea to herself, "but it doesn't matter, because there's more to me. I am not the person I was."

The warehouse doors were open, the basement was sunning itself, and the dust was settling. She left the large doors open. The mattresses were as flat as pancakes and dead as beds. The gloom had departed.

"Time to go and find my body and see what they've done," she said in a light-hearted way, running up the stairs two at a time.

# 13

# Eternal

Bea felt light, clear, and at peace with the world. There was a bounce in her step as she walked through the corridors and, every now and then she did a little skip. The hospital seemed a sunny, airy and beautiful place to be. When she saw the faces of anxious visitors, she felt compassion for them. *This feeling connects us. It's a warm feeling. You actually feel the warmth in your chest. How unexpected!*

Several times she considered cuddling a parent pacing down the sides of a ward waiting for diagnosis results, but it seemed a risky step to hug an unknown adult. She passed a 6-year-old boy sitting outside his brother's ward. He had a sports car still in its box sitting on his knee and tears in his eyes. She squatted down and put her hands on his knees and looked into his eyes. She wasn't bothered whether he would see her or not.

She said, "It's okay."

He looked at her soulfully. "I broke his car, and we couldn't get a new one the same. He doesn't want this one; it's not a Shelby Cobra."

"Never mind. You tried," she consoled him. "I wish you were my little brother."

He nodded.

"What's your name?"

"Justin."

"Well, that comes from the word justice," she explained, "and today you tried to do justice, just like your name."

Justin nodded.

"That's who you are."

He nodded.

"Can I have this Porsche Spyder then? My dad says I can't because I broke his on purpose."

Bea was out of her depth already. "Think that's up to your dad," she winced as she stood up.

"Well, I tried," she said to the Presence. "What is the word for that then?" *Encouragement*, she thought. *Well, there's a first time for everything!*

She found her ward easily. Her mum wasn't there. *I want to communicate with my mum properly. I want her to know I see her as a person, not just as my mum. That I appreciate her. She's so important to me, and she's a good mum. Of course, I have to get back in my body first, so Mum can hear me.*

Bea sat on the bed, next to her own body, holding her own hand. She had a big plaster and bruising around the nose and a bandage on her head. She seemed more fragile. Maybe she'd lost weight, or it could just be all the bruising. She looked at the monitor to see how she was doing, and saw something else in there too: Eternal's reflection as he stood behind her.

She rubbed her PJs pocket. Under the material she could feel the texture of the wage packet from Grandma's bakery and remembered that Ralphy's seeds were still in it. She was grateful it was there, reminding her, one day, she would be planting them in the kingdom. She treasured it thoughtfully.

"Maybe it's for the best," Bea said to her body, aware that Eternal was listening.

Eternal was dressed in a white suit and bowler hat with light spinning in his no-eyes. He was smiling. "Bea, you're very calm, your heart rate is surprisingly low, considering that you found Morgan and read his medical notes. You seem to have accepted the operation?"

Bea was lost in thought. *He's not from Earth. Eternal isn't defined by the universal rules; he walks through walls, floats, turns up in Vietnam and the classroom. He plays 'universal rules', because he can break them all. If I needed a rule, I could've just studied him. He wasn't in the kingdom. He didn't recognise Boundless. He doesn't fit there; he's too manipulative.*

"Where did you say you were from?" Bea turned to exam Eternal carefully.

"I didn't. I'm not defined by place. You seem ready to break your final universal rule, Bea."

*He seems real.* She looked at him through new, yet experienced eyes. *But he's stark, clear-cut and a little too defined.*

"Where's your Presence?" she queried.

"Your gift comes with your final rule. Are you ready?"

She turned back to arrange her own body's hair. "I just need to reflect on the final rule. Can you give me a little thinking space, please?"

"Your manner has changed," Eternal said suspiciously.

"Everything about me is different. I'm not the person I was."

"Your nature is the same, it's just tempered with skills, and your communication has increased beyond my estimates. Are you appreciating your growth?"

"Yes," said Bea with genuine sincerity. "I have grown."

"Outstanding!" Eternal was astonished. "You finally appreciate the incredible opportunity I am giving you to have a full and rich life. It's a rare gift." Eternal paused, aware something was missing. "Where's the sheep, Bea?"

Bea focused on Eternal. "Like I said, I grew up."

"Excellent!" agreed Eternal. "All right, thinking space," and he disappeared.

*Eternal has no Presence, but he's not dead. It's as if he's a projection of a larger tangible quality that isn't being displayed. Something, or someone, is behind him.*

She wasn't anxious as she lifted the bandage on her hair. There was the shaved mark already regrowing, and a little scar. The little scar had healed. In fact, when she compared it with Morgan's, her scar was older by several weeks.

She scrambled to the end of the bed. They had replaced the notes Boundless had eaten. Her operation was seven weeks ago, according to the notes, and eight out of the nine programmes had been completed successfully.

*Eight out of the nine programmes!* It snapped into place, the jigsaw was complete and the picture displayed. *It's not a programme of drugs! It's the universal rules; they're a program! It's Eternal. Eight out of the nine complete. He's in my head. He's ... inserted!*

The shock was registering. *The crash, the induced coma, they had already operated! All that time, from the first moment he appeared, he was already in my head! I was in the past, my mum agreeing to the operation, the nurses getting me ready to operate, even the classroom, it was all in the past. It has already happened! He isn't seeking permission, just acceptance of what they did without my permission, so I don't reject the program, like Morgan had. My heart rate is going up. Breathe.*

*The universal rules are just a game so my mind engages with the inevitable result and doesn't reject him. He's what? A chip? A computer program. No, he's adapting and sophisticated. Always ahead. A projection of something larger.*

*Urgh! I feel dirty and tainted. He's snuck inside, and attached himself, like head lice crawling under my scalp.* She shuddered and ruffled her hair furiously.

"You agreed," Eternal stood too close for comfort, leaning over her shoulder.

*And he's reading my thoughts!*

"I didn't know what I was agreeing to!" she gasped, spinning around. "You're a virus!"

"Your heart rate is peaking. Breathe, Bea." Eternal slid onto the bed next to her.

Bea felt as if she was going to pass out. She turned on him, "You're not having me!"

She reached to grip Eternal as he disappeared, anticipating the clumsy move.

"Breathe, Bea." His voice echoed in the room.

The monitor started an emergency beep, her heart rate reached critical.

Bea took the wage packet out of her pocket and held it in her balled-up fist. *I'm nutmeg in an egg flan. Breathe. Nutmeg in an egg flan. Breathe.* The faintest smell of nutmeg wafted into the room as Bea rocked herself on the bed, breathing it in deeply. The monitor relaxed into its normal pattern. A nurse ran in, flicking her eyes on the still patient. She checked the monitor and reset it, before leaving. *Nutmeg in an egg flan, big breath.* Bea put the packet back in her pocket. *This is why Presence sent me back – it's not finished! Big breath. Wow! I'm slowing my heart rate down, and calming my temper. My mum will be so proud.*

"I'm your future, Bea, your purpose and destiny!" Eternal's voice warned. "Reject me now and you won't live. Like Morgan."

"You killed him!" Bea raged. Bea's heart rate ascended.

Eternal reappeared through the ward door, "You killed Morales."

"You're a ... a ... a bomb inside my head," Bea stuttered, struggling again to breathe.

"Oh no, I'm much more sophisticated than that," expounded Eternal. "I am expansive, omnipresent, powerful growth, creative change and the hope of mankind. I have already solved the problems that each human grapples with: the crisis, the corruption of this planet. I am the answer before you seek it and I have given you the ability to communicate better than any person on this planet in ways you can't begin to dream of yet! Would you like to see?"

"No," said Bea, her breathing shallow as she struggled to control it. "No, get out! Get out or I won't do the last program. I'd rather die."

"I know you, Bea," said Eternal, as he leant against the ward door with a satisfied air, pleased that at last the blister had burst. "No, you wouldn't rather die, and I won't let you, not now we've come so far."

"I need to think. Leave," Bea demanded, slowing her breathing and her heart rate.

"No," said Eternal, pressing his advantage. "You've run out of time."

Bea tried to block him out of her head and breathe. She tried to think of Grandma's house and the smell of the bakery. But the picture wouldn't come. She tried to think of Boundless, but she just saw a sheep.

"I'm really impressed with your vocabulary choices," Eternal stated. "I gave you an extensive lexicon to choose from. Your cognitive functions of forethought, logic, creative thinking, reasoning, problem-solving and decision-making have improved immensely. So have your memory, retention, ability to compress and file information and to plan a course of action. You're able to articulate emotions verbally, use humour, decipher body language, perceive lies and your intonation and perception are enhanced. You have adapted these to include a wider spectrum of colour in your emotions and arguments. You are increasing the speed and clarity of your thought and accessing knowledge you were not aware you had, because you didn't have it." He smiled at her, "Now tell me, where did that all come from?" He tapped the side of his head. "You've grown, because you were given the capacity to grow. You'll wake up in your own body with that capacity and more."

Bea began to doubt.

Eternal sat on the chair and leant in. "I'm just here to help, Bea. To help you fulfil your destiny as the best person you are capable of being, and there is more to come!" he said with excitement.

Bea thought. What if everything she had experienced was down to Eternal trying to normalise a very autistic child?

"You said I was a psychopath."

Eternal smiled. "You were an autistic child with severe communication issues and some personality problems. Now you've a future ahead of you. Isn't it time to step into that?"

*My feelings are controllable now, and I do feel released, but your program didn't release me from them. It gave me skills, but it didn't change my heart. This can't just be some incredible artificial intelligence sorting my head out.* She caught sight of the monitor; her heartbeat was decreasing, her breathing had normalised, and underneath that the manufacturing logo: 'Astrostar Innovations'.

*Morgan's hospital monitor will be silent; his mum and dad will be crying as they leave the ward. Maybe they will have mixed feelings. He's not in a coma any more, not suffering with autism. They believe they lost their beautiful boy in a minibus crash.*

*They won't know that Astrostar Innovations caused the minibus crash, that the hospital placed their child needlessly in a coma and gave him the Eternal program he terminally reacted to. They don't suspect this company and others are connected to a world order that doesn't care whether people die, to fulfil their agenda. That the sky is burning and the reapers screaming with the injustice in a layer of the kingdom they don't know exists. That Presence sent me to rescue my classmates before their parents go through similar pain, even though I've no idea how to.*

She had empathy and Eternal didn't.

"What did it cost you to help me?" she asked.

Eternal was surprised by the question. "This is multi-million-dollar research at the forefront of AI."

"That's the excuse you're going to give Morgan's parent's when they find out how their child died in a crash that you set up?" She grilled him, standing up and stepping into the argument.

"What is that to you?" Eternal asked, exasperated. "You and Morgan were hardly friends. You've never really thought about anyone but yourself. You can't fight this progress. You have a little choice: face the future or die."

"You have little choice! That sums up your approach, doesn't it. You have little choice! So, apart from denying me freedom to make my own choices, what've you really given me? All the skills in the world won't cancel out freedom to make my own decisions." Bea probed. "You said I would get to judge if my destiny was good, before the ninth rule?"

128

"Is your conversation limited by childish TV sayings now? like "Wipe my pants with a toothbrush?" Eternal asked.

"Skills and abilities don't give me a good destiny. Are these overworked medical professionals in the hospital with all their skills happy? Orme and his cronies, are they happy? Are they having a good life? Really? How's it good?"

"Bea, you have no idea of the power I am about to grant you and what you can do with it?" Eternal explained, with increasing frustration.

"No," said Bea. "But I know it's cost Morgan's parents far more than it ever cost you. I've seen the past and I'm finally living in the present, and unless you show me the future, I'll never accept this program. You and I know that; because I don't trust it and I don't trust you, and that is what is needed: trust."

"There isn't a choice, Bea. It's checkmate."

"You think? Well, there's a flaw in your game." Bea's super-calm highway sifted through her possible manoeuvres pre-ordering her moves. "Because I understand I'm the guinea pig; that the other guinea pig failed. That there is a lot of finance invested in this little guinea pig and behind that dollar, there's a world order with an agenda on a timescale. It doesn't tolerate anyone who doesn't come up with the goods: it assassinates them. You must be running out of time to prove your expensive AI research works."

Eternal conceded, "To some extent, yes."

Bea built on her position to close in on her game. "If you want lots of other guinea pigs following this breadcrumb trail of yours out of their autistic classrooms and into your finely tuned computer games, you'll need to iron out the kinks. So, you need to work out how to get me over the last hurdle."

"Your problem is, I don't trust it and I don't trust you. Now, if I can step into a future knowing that what I've put my confidence in has genuine value, then there is a true partnership." *I've got him, because I'm demonstrating something much more valuable than knowledge and processes. What is it?*

"Wisdom," came the lexicon's reply.

*Well, wisdom is not skill or knowledge, and I didn't get it from you, Eternal.*

She played the best move she had: "Show me the future," she demanded. "There is an opposite to everything. I used the universal laws of attraction, repetition, gender, death, mind, vibration, cause and effect, connection and," she paused, more for effect, "I saw the past, but we don't get to see the future. I want to break that polarity and see the future."

"Brilliant, logical thinking and reasoning," said Eternal, putting his glasses on. "Rule nine: polarity. Everything has an opposite. Program complete. I will see you shortly." Eternal disappeared.

Bea sighed. *The move only gives me stalemate, but it gives me time.*

She opened the door to the hospital corridor. A white drone was hovering in the air, at face height. The drone rotated and scanned her.

"Seer," it said, and hovered away to the next door. Bea jumped back into her room and closed the door.

# 14

# The cleaner

Bea stroked the base of a glossy white plastic bed curved to fit the human form. It changed colour to a translucent blue.

*The ninth program is installing in my brain. All I've accomplished is time. I've no plan to rescue the kids at school or myself. I don't know how to sabotage something implanted in my brain and live. I need answers.*

On the end of the bed was the familiar red and white triangle logo of Chemoxic. *It seems they make just about everything now – medicines, plastic beds, chemical warfare.* There was no monitor or medical equipment, no paper notes, just a screen integrated into the plastic-coated wall requiring security access. The dividing board and additional bed had been removed, making the room spacious and empty. *This is no longer an overcrowded children's hospital, because there is either less children, less illness or more building. Um, which?*

The screen shone out a familiar logo of the three white stars circling the points of a triangle and, below, 'Astrouniverse Innovations'.

"I reckon more building. What do you think, Eternal? Seeing as we're about to be besties forever!" She caught her reflection in the window. She was pleased to find herself in crisp white hospital pyjamas instead of her old jellybean ones, but she seemed older in the eyes, as if some of her innocence had evaporated.

"Thanks for the upgrade," she said to the absent Eternal.

The sun was rising and Bea observed the streets below from her window. The little cobbled street had disappeared with Grandma's house in it and a high-tech hospital extension had been added. A shuttle plane with a small dolphin nose and little protruding fins stretched out like an eel squiggling its way through the streets. *It must use sensors to stop it bumping into buildings. It's definitely flying rather than on wheels.* She watched it squirm past the hospital and hover to a standstill. A ramp slid out and an usher steadied passengers down it. The shuttle plane had the chopper butterfly symbol on its nose.

"Everyone's profited from Vietnam, well into the future. Well, the companies anyway." She was aware her comments had gained a cynical undertone.

She stepped into the hospital corridor. All of the white plastic-coated walls had integrated screens at various points. The hospital was silent. She saw a camera turn to acknowledge her movement. The drone hovering at the end of the corridor returned to assess her again.

"Seer," it said.

"I see you too," she said, noting the logo of the cake with the piece cut out, and Radartrek Inc. underneath.

"The walkie-talkie has grown eyes and wings," she commented to Eternal.

There were no clocks, monitors, or nurses. It seemed that hospitals had become very minimal.

"No need for people; everything's got a microchip in it!"

*I'm beginning to sound like Arthur. I never got humour, but now I speak cynicism and sarcasm.*

"Thanks for that, Eternal. I'm not sure that's a mark in your favour."

*I'm starting to sound like the person I was before – angry with everyone and everything. I don't want to be that person again. I don't want to be bitter, jealous and ugly underneath. Blaming everyone. That's not who I am. I can grow up. I'm nutmeg – warm, spicy – and actually if you suck on one it's really disgusting!*

*Okay, it's my fault, I broke the universal rules, but I didn't have the full facts. I had no idea that colliding with Eternal would start an AI instillation in my head. But I didn't care, I just wanted to break rules and the floating was fun. Maybe this is my mess, but I didn't cause the minibus crash that got me here! I am responsible, at least for some of it.* She sighed. *I need help.*

She went to push through a smart automatic door. It was locked. A side screen lit up.

"Identify," said the screen.

*Is it triggered by body heat?* The three white stars logo flashed up. *How far into the future am I?*

"Good morning, Seer," the screen said it a smooth voice. The door opened.

*They're not recognising me they're registering the implant. I must've changed my name to Seer.*

Through the door another screen awakened and played an advert. A large young man was working into the night at his desk. He was eating a doughnut and a family bag of crisps.

A ridiculously cheerful voice said, "Struggling with too much carbs and sugar? Enrolment on our eating addiction app is at a record levels."

"No I'm not," scowled Bea.

The advert changed. A young woman was in the gym, pounding on a small punchbag. She turned to the screen: "Is anger and aggression taking over your life?"

She addressed the screen, "Really! Personalised advertising based on facial recognition, voice intonation and body mass?"

*The lexicon is integrated. Listen to my speech! Wow!*

The advert altered to a silicon woman sitting in an egg-shaped hanging chair, she nodded her head sympathetically "You don't need to struggle alone; a personalised counselling service is available."

"Get lost!" Bea shouted as she walked down the corridor.

The screen continued "Upgrade your personalised satnav here,"

*"Argggh"* Bea shouted. "It's brainwashing!" Bea stopped, breathed deeply, held her head up and tried to walk past the next

screen in a nonchalant, blank-faced manner. It revealed a clean, new factory in Bangladesh.

"Have you got spare finance credits. Check out the latest fashions, with full assurance that your clothes are made by workers on the universal pay grade. Modern slavery is a thing of the past thanks to Eternal."

She stopped and stepped back; the workers were waving. *What's Eternal doing now?* She moved cautiously back to the screen and waited.

"The tree-planting experience in Africa is gaining momentum as volunteers arrive from around the continent," the presenter smiled.

She saw people totally unprepared for African weather being handed a bottle of sun cream as they got off a shuttle plane.

"Spurred on by the desire for additional access credits, these volunteers are regrowing huge swathes of forest, supported by modern technology ..." the presenter explained. "Thanks to the combined efforts of Chemoxic, Radartrek and Astrouniverse Innovations."

*Well, they might as well be the same company now, if they're not already.*

As if on request, it rained onto a vast landscape of twig trees. A few soaking wet volunteers smiled at the camera as they plodded through the mud to collects more sticks from a truck. *The truck has the Astrouniverse logo on it.* Bea shook her head in disbelief and automatically the screen registered it.

"Disillusioned and depressed? Mercitane 325mg is now available on prescription, thanks to Chemoxic ..."

She arrived at the corridor stairs to find them recoated with white plastic, non-slip surfacing, and screens inhabiting the walls.

As she stepped down the levels, each screen recognised her and provided an advert.

The late-night crisp-eater returned to the screen "I can't buy chocolate, cake or crisps any more, I have all the self-discipline I craved. Thanks to Eternal," He jumped onto his desk and juggled broccoli.

Bea baulked. That was painful on so many levels. *Eternal can stop me eating chocolate? And make me eat vegetables? I hadn't considered the loss of choice over such simple things as what to put in my mouth!* She felt the temper of the old Bea rising at the very thought of it. *Breathe. He's trying to distract you. Keep focused. This can wait*, she told herself.

She walked down the steps to the next screen, using deep, purposeful breaths, hoping for a distraction.

"In Botswana, seed implantation is being delivered with six months' worth of nutritional supplements, and forty additional finance and health credits per person for the first three years. Demand has been so intensive we've had to open up this sports stadium to deliver this amazing service," the presenter gushed.

Queues of people were lined up everywhere in the stadium. The place was packed, and the people were dancing and singing like Christmas was there every day.

Bea was aware, mainly through Gran Tann's lectures, that life had never been just. Gran Tann explained that while she was stuffing her face with chocolate, another child born into a poor family on the other side of the planet, where the chocolate was grown, had never even tasted it. Now, for the first time, it seemed a fair point.

*I've probably eaten a lifetime's supply already. If a creamy chocolate bar appears on the table in front of me, I'll give it to the hungry child, sitting on the other side of the table. Well, I might ask for a piece, or I might try to share. I could do that; I could share it, fairly.*

"The planet is going to be greener. People are being paid a fair wage. Those with nothing are getting extra, and the rain comes on time. Sounds like it's going to be all sunshine and blue skies in the future," Bea said to a screen, knowing Eternal could hear.

As she walked into the corridor, two drones were sliding up and down the plastic walls, cleaning them. A cleaner stood in front of the basement door with a dirty little brown drone scooting near her. The cleaner wore a livid pink hospital uniform, against the white walls she stood out like a felt-tip stain on a school shirt. She was waving a duck-head implement as she argued with the screen.

"Zone twelve is not complete," said the woman on the screen. It was a good digital image, but the woman was not real. She had bouffant hair and was wearing the same clothes as the cleaner to encourage a sense of camaraderie and reduce isolation. The cleaner had not had time to coif her hair.

"You have ten minutes to complete. A helpful timer is on the top-right corner of your screen." Bouffant flicked her hand elegantly to the corner of the screen.

"Please ensure your container drone is in the appointed safety square." Slight pause. "Lois." The screen demonstrated this with a flourish.

The weary cleaner sighed as she looked at the brown drone. "The safety square is halfway down the corridor and I only have a helpful ten minutes!" she informed Bouffant.

Bea watched the cuddly older lady, limp towards her drone. From the tension in her voice, she was struggling to keep her cool.

"It is your duty to ensure safety. It is helpful to note that the container is a trip hazard. You have an 89 per cent safety record." Slight pause. "Lois, well done. Please do your best to maintain this," said the helpful Bouffant.

"After two days, an 89 per cent safety record, isn't good," Lois informed the screen, "because I have only reached a 42 per cent target, because I'm too slow at my job."

"Aim for a 60 per cent speed target rating. Take small steps to success." said Bouffant in her best encouraging voice. Slight pause. "Lois. You have 8 minutes and 43 seconds to complete your zone. Begin at the corner of your one-metre cleaning area." Slight pause. "Lois ...". The screen showed Bouffant graciously sliding her duck-head up and down the crease between wall and floor.

"I know! You've shown me at least fifty times. It's mopping!" Lois was losing it.

Bea was shocked because she recognised Lois's voice.

"Ensure an even pressure, by getting close to the crease between the wall and the floor."

A clock flashed on the screen: 8 minutes and 30 seconds.

"It would be helpful to increase your speed while maintaining your cleaning efficiency." Slight pause. "Lois," said Bouffant patiently.

Lois dipped her duck-head in the brown drone.

Bea was indecisive. She wasn't sure whether it was best to stay or retreat in this situation.

"Your service will ensure you receive health and finance credits, enabling you to celebrate working towards one people, one planet and one god." Slight pause. "Lois," and a white triangle appeared on the screen as Bouffant disappeared.

Lois muttered something very unladylike under her breath about what Bouffant should do.

Bea stepped forward. "What's the white triangle?" Slight pause. "Please."

Bea had caught her by surprise. Lois stepped back onto the drone, tipped the drone over, emptying the fluid contents onto the floor.

Bouffant reappeared on the screen. "There is a spillage in zone twelve." Slight pause. "Lois, this is your section. If a person has stepped onto your drone, please wipe the surface." Bouffant gracefully demonstrated. "Screens in the surrounding area will ensure all patients and staff are notified of the spillage." Bouffant flicked her hand to show the 'Warning spillage' sign. "Additional fluid will need to be collected from cupboard five." Slight pause. "Lois. The target time for the task will not be achieved," Bouffant added helpfully. "Please place the container in the ..."

"Safety zone," Lois interrupted.

Slight pause. "Lois," added Bouffant.

Lois kicked the drone purposefully; it wasn't its first dent. "Don't you hate it when it's right?" she smiled, addressing Bea and picking up the empty container.

"Would you mind if we step away from the screen?" asked Lois.

"Not at all, Miss Cotton," said Bea, delighted. She went to give her a hug and realised that Miss Cotton had no idea who she was. So, Bea examined her own feet.

"You must be a patient here?" Lois asked. "How do you know me? I haven't been called that for years. That's my maiden name," she laughed.

"How many years?" asked Bea.

"Oh, eight years in June." Bea looked at Miss Cotton; she looked older than that.

"I didn't teach you?" Lois asked, puzzled.

"You lived near us," Bea lied, "but I grew up." She added: "A bit."

"Not teaching then?" Bea asked, nodding at the bucket. *Why did I say that! That was the wrong thing to say! Talking with people is awful!*

"I'm not a cleaner either... um, what was your name?" Lois fished.

Bouffant continued giving directions to the absent Lois.

"Beattie, Beattie ... Roseacre." *Unconvincing*, thought Bea. *Too long a pause to think, and it's the name of my road! This isn't going well.*

"Oh yes, I remember you," said Lois, who clearly didn't.

Bea pressed on, "Miss Cotton, you taught autistic children, didn't you?"

"Are you lost? There are no wards down here. Shall I walk out with you?" Lois asked.

"Okay," said Bea, sensing Miss Cotton's agitation to get away from the screen.

Lois smiled and limped towards the door. Bea caught a glimpse in the smile of the person she'd once known, before her heart had sagged with her stature.

"Why did you stop teaching, Miss Cotton?"

"Shush," said Lois.

"Leaving your cleaning zone?" Bouffant had reset herself to the screen by the door. "Please ensure your equipment is stacked tidily in a safety zone ..."

Miss Cotton showed her wrist to the door and it automatically opened.

Bea looked back at the drone and duck-head strewn on the floor at the end of the corridor. It was clear Lois was not going back.

Bouffant followed them, like a friend that didn't get the hint. She was on the screen in the stairwell. "Please collect additional fluid from cleaning cupboard five before returning to zone twelve to complete the delayed task." Slight pause. "Lois."

Lois flicked her eyes up to the second stairwell and they walked up the stairs. "Are you seeking promotion?" asked the screen on the second stairwell.

"I have to go in this cupboard, for more fluid," Lois emphasised emphatically. "You need to go through that door and back to your ward," she said slowly, with her arm raised and her other hand pointing to the cupboard door. "Patients can't come in here," Then she nodded at Bea. Bea walked towards the stairwell door, dipped under the screen, and followed Lois into the storeroom, shutting the door.

The cleaner's room had some chemicals and a few duck-heads. She handed Bea an old drone to sit on and sat on an overturned bucket.

"I think if you talk slow enough, the screens can't decipher it," Lois explained.

"Really?" said Bea, wondering how Miss Cotton could believe such nonsense. Lois set the timer on her watch. "I have ten minutes, then security will arrive if I'm still in the cupboard."

*We have five minutes, then they'll know I'm in here, if they don't already!*

Lois grabbed Bea's wrists and checked them both. "Where's your parents?"

"I don't know," said Bea honestly. "What are you looking for?"

"Are you booked in for seed implantation?"

"No, I'm too young for babies"

Lois was shocked. "Where've you been hiding?"

Bea didn't have time to explain. "Miss Cotton, I need your help; I need to know what's going on? I've been hiding, kind of, and I just need some answers."

Lois nodded nervously.

"What were you looking for on my wrist?"

Lois presented her arm to Bea. It had three tiny bumps on the inside of her wrist, like three little seeds under the skin. The skin was tighter and lighter in the middle, forming a triangle. Each of the seeds had a minuscule tail where the implant had gone in. From Bea's angle, they looked like 999. She guessed, from Miss Cotton's direction, they would read 666.

"These are the seeds? The seed implantation? What do they do?" asked Bea.

"They're microchips." Lois pointed to each one on her wrist: "one for finance, that's got your banking, loan apps and finance credits on. One for health: it tells you your health credits and monitors your lifestyle. It has apps placed on it by your doctor. The last one is for access: it has your country ID, fingerprint records, your work and buildings access, and travel allowance. Everything is there, where your watch used to be, except of course the time. It's amazing really. Shopping, banking, work, life, everything is credit or debit. Of course, if you're in debit, you've nothing."

Bea felt her depression. "So, there's no money or cards? No fobs or keys? No choice if you mess up?"

Lois shook her head. "I didn't have a lot anyway, not after they came for the children at school."

"Why did they come?"

"Mr Orme brought a virus in with him, they'd found it on Bea and Morgan. We all had to go up to the hospital. The children never came back. They peeled those children off me," her eyes welled up with tears as the memory stirred strong emotions. "I'll never get over it. They were so frightened."

*This is what Presence showed me, I opened the floodgates. I accepted the program and they came back for my classmates. I don't know how to stop it.*

"Ralphy ...?" she stuttered.

"Oh, you know Ralphy? He was off school that day. I rang his parents, never saw him again," she laughed. "They gave me an injection and sent me away. I found Harvey in the forest, up a sycamore, eight o'clock at night. He'd been there all evening! They couldn't catch Harvey. Who could? A few weeks later I was out of a job. Then the world changed; the country went bust, the stock market went down and credits were introduced."

"What happened to your leg, Miss Cotton?"

"Harvey stayed at my house. His uncle was at the end of his tether with him, and I knew he'd just hand him in, so my mum and I hid him. He grew wild and frustrated hiding in the bedroom. One day, he made a bolt for the door. I pulled my knee out of its socket trying to hold him. I've not seen him since."

"Can't people say no to the seeds?"

Miss Cotton laughed. "Why would they? That's like saying no to money, food, healthcare, your kids, your home, your life! We placed all our information online. Everyone typed an @ sign into their email address. We did our passports, our NHS information, job applications, criminal record checks, all our banking – it's all online. All our proof that we exist, is online. To access it now, you had to have the implants. We didn't realise."

"Realise what?"

"We traded our freedom. Friends knew I was in trouble; they couldn't help. You can't pass the credits on – it's not like money. You can't collect for the office leaving do, pass on a parking ticket, give a gift. It was so hard to hide Harvey. Everything in your wrist is a map of what you're doing. It can zero your finance, and you starve. You can't skive off work; the health seed monitors your temperature, heart rate, breathing. It can zero your healthcare; you can't see a doctor or dentist. It can zero your access so you can't get through this cupboard door."

"And the 'It' is Eternal?" Bea asked, guessing the answer.

Lois nodded.

*This is the real Eternal. He steals choice, freedom and generosity, What's left?* She stood up, feeling tainted by the future. *I've overstayed.*

Lois snatched her hand, "I can't let you go. I need the credits. They're on their way. My neighbour sold his kidney last week."

*That's why my instinct was shouting at me to get out of the cupboard.* Bea felt gutted, betrayed by a person she'd respected and relied on to keep her safe. Bea's first reaction was to stamp on Lois's knee and knock it out of its socket again! *But what would that solve?*

"You handed Harvey in! You'd had enough of the squeeze on your purse! And him messing up your bedroom! Do the right thing Lois: let me go."

Lois hesitated. "I can't. I've no finance credits. I can't do this job. You're a winning lottery ticket. It's 1,000 credits if you find an unseeded person now. I can't keep cleaning!"

Bea shook her head with outrageous disappointment. "You'd never have let anyone take those kids, and you handed Harvey over for finance credits! What happened to your heart, Miss Cotton!"

Lois relaxed her grip and Bea strode out of the cupboard. Security stood outside waiting for her.

"Lois here found me," she said to the security guard, as Lois sheepishly left cupboard five. "She needs some financial credits adding to her account. She deserves it. She was a good teacher once, one of the best!" Bea said, grimacing.

The security guard was a large teenager with shades on. He boomed "Freeze," and Lois froze on the spot. A white triangle sign with a rotating eye in the middle of it appeared on the screen.

Bea turned back to Lois, "Don't be too hard on yourself; we all betray someone. I've done it most of my life, every time I put myself first, and their needs last." Lois's hurt welled under her eyes and a tear ran down her cheek. She was completely frozen. "See?" Bea sighed. "He can shut down your nervous system, but he can't freeze your emotions."

Bouffant reappeared on a square on the screen, "Return to zone twelve and complete your assignment." Slight pause. "Lois."

The guard had taken off his sunglasses to reveal dark, swirling shapes in his frosted eyes. He was gaping at Bea because she was still moving.

"Unseeded, stairwell five, second floor," the security guard stuttered to the screen. The screen flashed back a brief red-light warning. She heard the click of the doors locking. *If I make it up the stairs, I won't be able to access the next door.*

"Bring her to the security office." A face appeared on the screen wearing sunglasses. She recognised the American drawl immediately, despite the fact his voice had broken.

"Arthur?" she gasped.

# 15

## Arthur

The teenage guard marched Bea down the hospital corridor as Bea considered Miss Cotton, still frozen in the stairwell. She was chewing on her thoughts, as if she was scratching an itch inside her head. *There are people who care for children like teachers and parents. Some are very competent and nurturing and I wonder why my mum isn't like that. Some are completely incompetent to the point of neglect, and I'm just grateful my mum isn't like that. Then there's the reality of my mum. I live with her strengths and difficulties. Miss Cotton was a shining star, a competent anchor in the storm of life, a teacher who gave her all. She rescued Harvey and nurtured him in her own home. So, why did Miss Cotton change? Or was that selfish side always lurking underneath? Was Miss Cotton's cuddle real? Or was it frothy bubbles to cover the darker water of a person who wanted an easy life? Why didn't someone tell me people have an underneath to their surface? What is that called?*

"Character," the Eternal dictionary immediately replied to her from inside her brain. *And an underneath to their underneath?* "Values," said the lexicon.

Bea assimilated the information. *Have my character and values changed or are they just lurking underneath?* She tried to assess herself. She'd handled the betrayal differently. Surely that was a good sign? She hadn't just thumped Lois.

The teenage guard was very tense as he escorted his prisoner and had a tight grip on her arm.

"Ow," Bea complained.

He gripped tighter. *He's anxious, must be new to his job.* He was wearing a bulletproof vest, and black, army-type clothes and boots. His black cap and shoulder had braiding embroidered on it. *Nope he's already been promoted.* On his chest was the triangle with the eye in the middle. The screen next to the door interrupted Bea's scrutiny as a bubbly, busty girl in her late teens winked at them: "Tired of online schoolwork?" Busty asked "Why not join me and my friends in our exclusive chat room? Only ten additional school credits."

The guard scowled.

As the door opened, a pale teenage lad appeared on the next screen. "Check out the latest Manx Island Rally Series, for a knockdown price of one additional school credit per one-hour session."

"Oh, you haven't got any additional school credits?" Bea asked him.

"Not enough!" grumbled the guard.

"If my social life is tied to my school work, I'm doomed!"

"Aren't we all," groaned the guard, and his grip relaxed slightly.

The guard waltzed her through double doors and into a main corridor. She took the opportunity to examine his wrists for seeds – he didn't have any.

They passed a screen: "Struggling with rebellious thoughts?" it asked. "Try our youth citizenship app."

"Facial recognition, perfect for picking up defiant thoughts, eh?" Bea laughed.

The guard returned his tight grip.

She looked at her fresh wrist, with no seeds in them. *How would I feel to wake up and know even the number of steps I make is recorded? Same as a chip in my head, I guess: invaded. Will I be able to make generous choices, live spontaneously, think creatively, rebel? No, I won't. That's why Ralphy gave me the three seeds! It wasn't a present: it was forewarning!* She felt for the pocket to clutch Ralphy's seeds, but the white PJs didn't have a pocket. *How did Ralphy know I'd visit the future? Presence told him. The kingdom is more tangible and alive than this future. Nothing is hidden from Presence.*

"Thanks to Eternal …" the screen next to the door chirped. "Off," said a commanding voice. The white triangle on the screen faded into a pin prick.

"Ah, that's how you switch him off," said Bea to the absent Eternal.

"Only if you're a Seer," drawled Arthur. She twirled around to see grown-up Arthur, in his black uniform, waiting in what resembled the guard's locker room. The white plastic-coated lockers were floor-to-ceiling down one side of the room with a series of numbers on them, smudged and scratched from excessive use. There was a drinks station with its usual spilt coffee, dripping tea bags and bin full of wrappers, next to a few chairs and a table.

An entire wall of the locker room incorporated multi-screen images from all the hospital cameras. On the left-hand side, a list of names appeared and disappeared as people clocked in and out of the building. She spotted Miss Cotton's camera on one of the squares; she was still frozen in the stairwell.

"Not much of an office then, Arthur," Bea sneered, before she could stop herself.

"Your sarcasm won't help you here," Arthur said. His face was serious and his tone official.

"Really! Well, hasn't everyone changed!" she replied. Arthur had changed. He was pushing 20, he'd bulked out from the weed he used to be, with a bit of a paunch from too many movies and chocolate bars. He had a slim moustache and a grimace that meant business.

The teenage guard put his hands together to form a triangle and did a small bow. Arthur did a slack version, because he was the higher-ranking officer.

"Every army has to have a salute, so you can tell who's on your side!" Bea said sardonically.

"I am Captain of the Seer, Eighth Division," Arthur announced.

"I thought you'd do better, Arthur the Hacker."

"You can't pull your thread of familiarity here," said Arthur, doing his best to impress with his newfound seriousness, but obviously annoyed by the lack of impression he was making.

"I had an infamous younger life, everyone knows it. But pre-Eternal ties won't help you, little girl, so don't bother to lie," he said patronisingly. "You look a bit like Beattie Tanner, but she was fatter than you at your age. Are you related?"

*The cheek!* Bea felt an urge to thump him already. *He's going to ask for my name. Presumption – there's a new skill.* Having identified it, she filed it under 'communication achievements'. *Wow, my brain is so organised.*

She introduced herself, "I'm Rose Melon." *Melon! Couldn't you think of something better; you don't even eat melon!*

"Why aren't you seeded, Rose?" queried Arthur, rubbing his moustache.

"I'm a bit of a rebel, like you," she needled.

Arthur showed no signs of cracking into a laugh or regaining his sarcasm. He rubbed the side of his left leg, an attempt to hide an old stim.

"They've made you into a robot, then?" she said, hoping to get under his skin.

Arthur took his glasses off, in a bid to impress her with his black shapes swirling in his frosted eyes. "Sit down," he commanded.

"I'll stand," she said. "Are your classmates all like you Arthur?"

She flicked her eyes to Miss Cotton, still frozen on a screen square. *She's been static for at least 15 minutes. That must hurt, and you've just left her there.*

Arthur grasped her wrists and checked for imbedded seeds. "Unseeded found in Zone five," he reported proudly to the screen.

"Check for Ethical status, Seer status and take to relevant station. Well done, Captain, you are doing an excellent job. Your status is currently being reviewed," said a voice that sounded like Eternal's.

Bea clocked Arthur smiling to himself. *You're not all robot, then? Still some pride left in there.*

"Excellent job!" she said. "But you're taking someone else's credit: Lois Cotton captured me, and she's still frozen in stairwell five, second floor." *It's really satisfying to wind you up, especially when you're desperate to be professional.*

Arthur twitched a little. "Release Lois Cotton and give her 100 credits," he said to the screen.

"I thought it was 1,000 credits? Where will the 900 go?" she interrupted.

"She'll get those when you've been seeded," he answered politely. "Do you have any objections to the world order?"

"The what?" she said, waiting to hear his explanation.

"One people, one world, one god?" asked Arthur. A central screen enlarged to helpfully demonstrate the white triangle and its three points: one people, one world, one god. "Eternal Unity, order for the world," it explained underneath.

It struck her like lightning out of the multi-screen. Bea sat down. *This is the idea that unites the world order. That focused their decisions to create war and kill presidents. One people, one world, one god. They knew they could trigger financial collapse, and exchange money for credits. They invested in technology, pharmacy and surveillance companies. Now they control health, finance and access. They can manipulate unity using seed implantation and Eternal! An extensive AI facility. It was in the manufacturing logos all along – they all use white triangles! Brazenly advertising world order to those who know its significance.*

She regained composure, a little too late. "They just used to call it peace," she said dismissively to Arthur.

"Do you have any religious, ethical or moral objections that would stop you being seeded?" asked Arthur calmly and without effort.

The corporal had defrosted Miss Cotton and was escorting her out of the building. Her face was glum. *Guilt, that's the emotion she's expressing. That's my emotional recognition integrated!*

Bea tightened the screw of honesty a little. "You used to hack into the school's system, now the world system has hacked into you! Where's that got you, Arthur? Why've you got Eternal's eyes?"

Arthur stuttered slightly, as if the little part of himself in the back of his brain couldn't get to the front to talk. "Do ... do you understand and agree with the vision?"

"Is there a choice?" asked Bea. "Can I really choose to disagree with it?"

Arthur returned to his assessment checklist.

"Lean your head this way, please." He took a small scanner from his pocket and brushed it round the side of her head where her scar would be and it beeped. "You're a Seer?" he said. "But you never finished the program?"

Bea caught her breath. *Will you understand the truth?* "Do you remember the autistic unit, Arthur?"

Arthur was unflustered. He searched her eyes and concluded: "You've nearly finished the download. So, let's work out what's stopping you. You've time to accept the inevitable and embrace Eternal. Do you realise how powerful you'll be?" He rubbed the side of his leg as he pondered her.

"No," said Bea, drawing him out.

"Bring up Ward Seven," Arthur commanded the screen. The screen delivered the camera images for the ward, and placed them in the centre of the screen. It was a large ward with five children lying in beds, and on the bed nearest the screen, two parents were chatting to their child.

"Map," instructed Arthur. A map enlarged to show the movement of people around the hospital. She saw a triangle and eye symbol denoting a Seer not far from Ward Seven.

"Ged, can you enter Ward Seven."

"Yes Captain," came the reply from off the screen.

"No, don't do this!" said Bea, dreading what it might take for Arthur to prove his point. "Remember the autistic unit? How you hacked Orme's computer?"

Ged had arrived on the camera focused on Ward Seven. He didn't look old enough to be working.

"See the parents, tell them to grab one hand of the child each and pull in opposite directions," Arthur instructed. Ged took his dark glasses off.

"No!" begged Bea.

Arthur turned around, "Ready for a bit of respect, young lady?"

"Yes! Yes!" implored Bea.

"Pause them Ged," said Arthur. The parents and children were frozen. They looked terrified.

Arthur reeled around to her with the full force of a tangible authority, "Now, do you really want to be the victim of that power? Or will you be controlling it?"

Bea hid her eyes to regain herself under the unfolding situation. She peeped out. "But you've lost something, Arthur," she pleaded. "You've lost yourself. You were so rebellious and sarcastic and patronising and superior, a bit of an aloof idiot, but you were yourself."

"I'm just a different version of myself," Arthur stated securely. "I'm fulfilling my destiny; the world is changing and I will be helping to create that change."

"Release them, Ged. It was a demo," he said to the screen.

"Yes, Captain," Ged replied, and the couple and child relaxed momentarily, before clinging to each other like terrified chickens released from a fox. Ged reapplied his glasses, grinned at the screen and it minimised.

"Bring up Bangkok," Arthur directed. "Do you know that we have found over 170,000 missing people since the seed implantation began?"

A live screen enlarged. It displayed semi-naked, emotionally broken women and children getting into an ambulance.

"These women and children," Arthur pointed to the screen, "they were being exploited by sex traffickers." Arthur was considering Bea's age. "Most of these are younger than you. You're aware what I'm saying, here?"

150

Bea nodded, and looked at her armpit. She didn't want to talk about sex.

"This is live. We sent two Seers into the vicinity, and these victims were automatically released, because the traffickers knew the consequences."

"These children cry with gratitude at being seeded; they feel safer tagged onto our satellite system. We've been doing this to our dogs and cell phones for twenty years. Now ask yourself: that child crying with relief at being found, isn't she worth more than a dog? Do you want to see the mother's reaction when her child is brought back to her?"

Bea shook her head.

"No, you don't. No one wants to see that kind of heartbreak!" Arthur rubbed his leg vigorously to reduce his emotion. He paused.

*He's seen too much*, Bea empathised.

On the screen, a man swaggered out of the building with his hands up. The local Bangkok police had him on the ground and surrounded him with guns.

"This is the lead trafficker handing himself in. We don't have to send them through any justice system; it's too expensive. They'll be seeded on the spot. They're criminals."

"Highlight the Seer," Arthur instructed. The screen highlighted a young woman, no more than 15, wearing the same uniform as Arthur, standing across the road from the action, with two guards. "She's wired directly to Eternal. She can ask Eternal to zero or delete anyone with a seed – his mother, father. He can watch their credits disappear. His mother won't be able to access any medical facility, his father will have no finance, they won't be able to open their own front door. They know there's no future without Eternal. He's already won. Everyone wants to access food and use a toilet. We don't need to carry weapons; once they're seeded, we are the weapon."

One of the ambulance crew approached the trafficker and opened a small bag.

"There, he's being seeded. He'll not commit a crime again, or we may arrive to help him kill himself."

The screen minimised and Arthur focused on Bea.

"Isn't that the justice we all long for? Freeing kids from exploitation, ensuring the corrupt start to work honestly, instead of leeching off other people? A safe, free world for all? Don't you see yourself as an exposer of exploitation, fighting for the innocent, Bea?"

Bea saw the appeal. Corruption on an unprecedented scale was finally getting its just deserts. The flying harvesters in the kingdom would soon be sitting by a red beach enjoying ice cream, the pain and suffering of a cruel world diminished by a new world order.

"But it's a big responsibility." Arthur flipped a chair around and sat down. "That's why I'm not sarcastic, or hacking the system or thinking I'm the big man. I'm playing my part in creating justice. Now wouldn't you rather do that?"

Bea felt a little small. She'd underestimated him. He wasn't bad in his eyes; he was fair.

"Why autistic kids?" Bea queried.

"You know the answer to that really." Arthur leant back into familiar territory. "You know us: we're more honest; less deceptive; less, if any, empathy; self-focused." He stretched out and relaxed. "Autistic people are less inclined to maintain relationships, friendships or family commitments. Many of us can spot one error in thousands of true records. Some of us have an astute understanding of manipulation, like you Rose. We've a strong sense of justice, are less likely to engage in corruption and we feel safe in order."

He looked at Bea earnestly. "If you're young enough to adapt to this," he tapped the chip side of his head, "and you can manage the brain adjustments, you get to restore order."

"Brain adjustments, so we can communicate and function?" Bea added.

"Pretty much," Arthur agreed.

"How do we freeze the seeded, Arthur?"

"Fourth chip is in the base of the neck. It overrides the nervous system, makes them freeze. It's a security system too; it registers tampering. That's important or criminals would just chop a hand off to gain access, wouldn't they? We can make the seeded do most physical things. It's difficult to refuse, but not impossible. They can't resist for long," Arthur stated, matter-of-factly. "You don't get to use it much," he sighed with disappointment. "Most people see it used once and never want to see it again."

Arthur assessed his impact on her. He leant forward. "Seems extreme? It keeps our families safe too, Rose. Practically all of the kids in this hospital triggered an automatic ambulance. Sometimes the ambulance arrives before their parents know the child is ill. The health seed detects temperature, heart and blood pressure, sugar levels, fits, depletion in oxygen. It tells us if they're dying. We can get there faster, and we know if it's a genuine emergency! Saves resources!"

"Have you seen enough to make a sensible decision, Rose?" Arthur asked, as if he was her big brother.

"I think so, but could I see one more thing before I change?"

Arthur nodded. "Doubters always want to see the alternatives."

"Thanks Arthur. You've become a better person than I thought possible."

They stood up to go.

"Arthur, was Beattie Tanner a good Seer?"

"Ah, I thought you were related!" He smiled, pleased with his breakthrough. "She was the first. She was okay. It's harder being the first, I think. She was iconic. If she hadn't made it, they might have struggled to justify sending more children through the process. Morgan died."

Bea noted the past tense. "How did she die?"

"An unseeded person stabbed her last week. They executed him on the spot. She was a bit old for the transition program, had a bit of compassion – that's worth learning from." He studied her; she was listening. "He was hiding his unseeded lover, an autistic man, too old and unsuitable for a Seer. He's Beattie's ex-classmate, I guess that's why she tried to intervene. He's booked into the seed centre." He paused, thinking his own thoughts.

*Is it Ralphy or Harvey?* Bea thought.

"Funny," said Arthur, smiling. "Beattie gave me pretty much the same talk I'm giving you. You do remind me of her."

"Yeah, but I'm slimmer," Bea smiled.

# 16

# The seed centre

*Why does everything have to change?* Bea sighed. The basement was transformed. The dankness of old mattresses and dusty broken equipment had been revitalised into a huge white reception area, with a shuttlebus bay outside. The warehouse doors had been renovated into smart doors on the right and smart revolving doors on the left. It had reception booths along both side walls. Along the top of the wall was a sign: "the Granary". It was an apt name for a seed centre.

The white walls had images of forests and mountains and waterfalls and other serene, calming images projected onto them. A children's area had cartoons projected on them and, as they were life-size, you could pretend to join the cartoon. *That's cool!*

The doors were manned by guards. They had no sunglasses, but they had guns. Arthur was vigilant and a little edgy. *The last of the unseeded queue up here and the Seers are powerless without implanted seeds. It's a great place for a riot.* She noted that the people walked in through the smart rotating doors but went out through the smart automatic doors, using a seeded wrist. *So, without a seed implant, you can't get out.*

A message flicked onto the wall – the huge white triangle outlined in red. The three points of the triangle explained "one people, one world, one god". Then, in the middle of the triangle, it said "Eternal Unity."

"So, Eternal's now god?" she asked Arthur, tongue in cheek.

"He is," said Arthur, "and we're better for it."

Arthur spoke to a security guard with seeds on his left wrist and a rifle in his right. *I guess they're implanted in your non-dominant hand, so you can hold something while using your seeds.*

"Let her explore where she wants. She'll ask to be back in the clinic shortly," Arthur explained to the guard. "She has two hours max. When you finish your shift, bring some snacks from the vending machine up to the Seers' security room." Arthur winked at her, "Perks of the job!"

The guard nodded with recognition, and saluted Arthur by forming a triangle with his free hand at the side of his head. Arthur gave an informal triangle salute back, said something to the screen and left.

Bea's face appeared on a screen next to the guard. She side-stepped the camera to find it was following her. She didn't like being watched it was uncomfortable. A teenage icon appeared on the screen. "Don't pick your nose," he said. "You have just been highlighted."

"I don't want to be," said Bea, squirming. She trotted into a queue of people in the hope she could hide from the camera.

A flying shuttlebus arrived and more people navigated the revolving doors, queuing at the reception areas. The queues had a low, depressing feel, not the same as the African party Bea had witnessed in the stadium. These were the dregs of unseeded that had been transported there against their will. They shuffled about, lost and resigned. *This feels like something from the Holocaust, in a bright shiny environment.*

A large screen hanging from the centre showed a happy young nurse and a concerned older patient. "Do remember the actual implant process takes less than five minutes. You will experience a brief moment of pain with each seed implant." The screen demonstrated the implants going in and the older person patiently smiling.

"It may be sore for the next two days. If there is any sign of infection, please visit your doctor immediately. There are no long-term side effects."

Another presenter came on, walking down a forest lane as if he was talking about farming concerns and forestry techniques. He continued: "You will be able to use your seeds immediately. Ensure you have photographic proof of your ID ready; this will be incinerated on completion. Your bank details will be checked and once your finance seed is implanted, your bank card will be destroyed. If you're a British resident, your health number will already be on the system, but please make sure you have proof of your national insurance number with you. Existing credits can be examined at the beginning of the process and on completion, for your reassurance."

Another presenter in a headscarf appeared: "Foreign nationals will need to queue in the lane marked for them. Do not worry; you will be reunited with your loved ones once the process is complete, as long as you clear the relevant visa or immigration status authorisation. Refugees will be removed to the refugee facility. Please do not be alarmed if you see this happen while visiting the Granary. It is to ensure immigration status is confirmed."

The forest man returned: "Should you decide not to continue with the seed implant, you will be offered counselling before your final decision is made. Counsellors and counselling rooms are available at any time. Do ask if you need to see one."

A woman presenter holding a baby smiled and waved the baby's wrist. "All babies are now seeded in maternity wards, ensuring a safe, secure future for your baby."

People were giving each other plenty of space in the queue. *There aren't many children, just a few toddlers. I guess seed implantation went into schools, in the same way as every other injection.*

She watched the queue and saw the screens ask each person for their decision. An occasional, resolute, proud person chose not to have the implants. Their bravery faded with the strength in their legs as they wobbled towards the counselling door.

She observed some hesitating before the screen, lost in indecision, between their moral high ground and reality. Once they had resolved to accept the seed, everyone examined their passport. *Maybe they are reliving their holiday memories, or more likely saying goodbye to their perception of themselves*. The screens chivvied them on to place their ID in the slot to be inspected before incineration.

A nurse waited in a booth by the side of each reception area. The person sat in a chair and placed their non-dominant arm on the screen in the table and the three seeds were efficiently inserted.

The nurse turned the chair around and placed the final seed in the back of the neck. This one seemed to hurt more, as it connected to the nervous system, and they usually flinched. They placed their seeded wrist back on the table. It confirmed the seeds' data and that the security implant was working. They were asked to confirm their credits were correct. There was a moment of "lostness and adjustment" as they left the nurse's chair. By the time they showed their wrist to the smart exit door to board the shuttle, they had already got their chests out and heads high, convincing themselves they'd done the right thing and there was no other choice anyway.

To one side of a queue a young woman with "water technician" written on her jacket was refilling a water station. She was uncomfortable being in the Granary. A counsellor appeared at the front of the queue and walked a confident young woman toward the doors at the far end of the basement. She held her head high. The water technician watched.

"She won't be back," Bea heard a middle-aged woman behind her mutter. The ones who walked through the counselling doors often didn't come back. Some did, looking crestfallen, burdened with a guilt and shame that might linger forever. The water technician was tinged with it too.

Bea was trying to work out the percentage of people that went to the counselling rooms, but she was distracted by a small commotion at the front of a queue. The guards didn't rush to investigate. Bea moved up to the front of the queue to see what happened. She was waiting for someone to shout, "Oy! What are you doing? Get to the back of the queue," like they did in the supermarket, but no one said a thing. It was very quiet and unsettled.

"Do you have any religious, ethical or moral objections that would stop you being seeded?" the screen said calmly and kindly, with the words appearing as it spoke. "Please speak clearly or tap the screen's yes/no buttons."

"987," said the man.

"Ralphy?" said Bea.

Ralphy turned round, his head cocked on one side and looked at Bea, his eyes searching her soul to see if she was still there, somewhere.

"It's Bea," she whispered. "Hello Ralphy," she said, giving him a big hug.

Ralphy stiffened. He looked confused and suspicious, but he was getting a hug. He was a skinny and very tall young man and his hair was starting to thin near the temples.

"Do you have any religious, ethical or moral objections that would stop you being seeded?" the screen repeated calmly and kindly.

Ralphy turned around and headbutted the screen. "988!" he said.

*Ralphy would definitely benefit from Eternal's communication program. He's frustrated, he speaks a number language no one else understands! Eternal could've been an amazing opportunity for him.*

Ralphie pressed the "yes" button.

"Ralphy, you've just pressed 'yes'. Are you sure about that? Do you have an objection?" Bea asked Ralphy.

Ralphy pushed Bea back without looking at her and again pressed "yes" to confirm his objection.

"Is it moral, religious or ethical?" came the tick-box reply from the screen.

Ralphy ticked all three.

"Are you a Christian?" asked the screen in its superficial, kind and helpful voice.

*It isn't a coincidence that I've arrived at the seed centre at the same time that Ralphy is checking in. Either Arthur arranged it to help me accept the transition to Seer. Or Eternal did, to try to help me lose empathy, so I don't die in a few years at the hands of Ralphy's lover.*

Ralphy pressed the "yes" button.

"A counsellor is available. Would you like to talk to a counsellor?"

Ralphy was shaking again.

"Do you know what you're agreeing to? Talk to a counsellor, Ralphy!" Bea jumped towards the screen and pressed the "yes" button and a counsellor appeared from a room behind the reception area.

"Good morning. Would you like to come with me please," the counsellor asked, not expecting a reply. Ralphy scowled at Bea, but he followed her toward the counselling room.

"Are you a family member?" the counsellor asked Bea.

"Seer," she said.

The counsellor stopped. She was an uptight woman in her late thirties with a rigid posture and an unfriendly face with her best effort at a smile plastered on top. Her hair, like the rest of her, had refused to calm itself completely and stuck out at strange angles. She tried to pat her hair down but it bounced up. She remembered to do a formal triangle salute to Bea, and wrung her hands.

"Not finished my program yet," Bea explained apologetically, not bothering to salute back.

The counsellor guided Ralphy through a door and Bea followed. The counsellor accessed a screen with a wave of her wrist.

"You have twenty minutes of my time. I am completely impartial and here to help you make a decision you are content with," the counsellor explained to Ralphy, gesturing that he should sit on a white seat.

*Well, that's all lies.*

Ralphy scowled again at Bea at the thought of suffering the counsellor. "5," he said to her.

"Out of ten?" Bea replied.

The counsellor returned to the screen. "Beach scene," she said, and the walls were washed with sea and sand and Ralphy and the counsellor's seats had a stripy blue and white deckchair effect.

The counsellor sat down and leant forward in practised earnestness, "I see, Ralphy, that you're undecided whether to have the seeds?" She used a calm, practised, low counselling tone, spiced with false concern, a tilt of the head and many nods.

Ralphy shook his head.

"You've decided?" she nodded and nodded.

Ralphy replied with a nod.

Bea was pacing, "He's autistic. He only communicates in numbers."

The counsellor was agitated that Bea was there interrupting, but wary. "Um, thank you. If you could allow me to continue."

She started to speak slowly and gestured with her fingers to her wrist, "Do you want the seeds in your wrist for food, and medicine and finance?"

Ralphy shook his head. The screen recorded Ralphy's decisions. Bea watched it like a clock.

"Do you know that you can't access food, medicine or college or work without the seeds?" the counsellor continued.

Ralphy nodded. "51,"

"He's obviously not right. He's just lost his boyfriend and he's grieving!" said Bea, pacing.

Ralphy scowled at Bea and banged his head with his hand.

"You're not helping him," said the counsellor, as if there was grit in her teeth. "He has no alternative but to select an option. Those who cannot decide do not return. Understood?"

Bea understood. *This is his last chance, either way. The counsellor is trying to save his life.*

"Do you understand, Ralphy, that you will die without the seeds?" said the counsellor, returning to the false sincerity, tip of the head and the nodding.

Ralphy did a little nod and turned and glared at Bea, as if to say, "Don't interrupt!"

"It would be unkind to let you die of starvation. We allow you to die here at the centre instead, quickly," the counsellor said.

Ralphy knew. He nodded.

"No," said Bea. "No." Her shoulders sagged at the helplessness of it all. She leant against the wall for support.

Ralphy looked daggers at Bea, as if to say, "Don't deny me my right to decide for myself."

"Are you selecting to die rather than take these three small seeds and have them inserted in your wrist?" The counsellor held them in her hand.

Bea remembered Grandma's and the three small seeds Ralphy had placed in her hands and knew this was why; it was for this moment. "Oh, Ralphy, I remember," she said, as her body slid down the wall into a squat.

Ralphy turned around and saw her. He smiled the biggest beam. *He's electing to go home.*

Ralphy nodded and tapped the woman's hands away and the three seeds scattered onto the white plastic floor.

"23." Ralphy grimaced his teeth together as if in pain. "Yes," he said. The screen recorded his reply.

Bea's insides crumpled. *Of course Ralphy would choose the Kingdom. Everything is incredibly generous, because Presence is. Why wouldn't he? Everyone appreciates each other and unconditionally recognises the presence of every citizen. Everyone loves.*

She watched Ralphy sign the screen and knew that something beautiful was leaving the world. He turned around to look at Bea. His big blue eyes looked sad and then he smiled a bright, courageous smile that said, "It's done. I'm going home. No more hiding."

Another door opened at the back of the counselling room and the counsellor signalled for Ralphy to go through. Bea went to follow.

The counsellor put her hand out to stop her. "Don't touch me," Bea snapped. "Tomorrow I will be a Seer." The woman stepped back.

"Sorry, I was just trying to protect you. You're a child," the counsellor stuttered.

"Not any more," breathed Bea, blinking the tears from her eyes. She followed Ralphy.

*Here's choice fading in front of me. Where's the second chance? To mess up, to run from your past, to face your mistakes and start again. Miss Cotton used to say, "Make good choices," but if I didn't, I got another chance. Now there's no more second chances.*

The back door had opened into a corridor of mirrors. *Why mirrors? So the last thing you see is yourself, and change your mind?* The counsellor walked Ralphy down the corridor and into one of the many doors opposite.

*Every mistake is itemised on a seed and has to be corrected with credits – who can be that perfect? Eternal gave us enforced justice and safety, at the cost of something even more integral to who we are: Presence. Of course, Ralphie can't give it up, because he's full of it.*

The counsellor instructed Ralphy, in an official tone, "Take off your shirt, please. You have ten minutes and a person will come through this door coloured red." She waved her hand at the door and left, unaware she was saying goodbye to the bravest person Bea had ever known.

*How can freedom to love exist at the same time as the unforgiveness of no second chance? Love exists because we all get to choose to not love too, otherwise, it's not love, is it?*

Ralphy looked up into Bea's face and smiled sadly. He took his shirt off and went down on his knees.

"Don't knock yourself out now, Ralphy! They're coming for you. You've minutes!" pleaded Bea. "I don't know what to do or say, Ralphy."

He opened his hands out, lifted his head up, closed his eyes and smiled. She watched him for a moment, waiting, but he just knelt there.

*He's praying.* Bea couldn't ever remember praying. He looked beautiful with his skinny chest and thinning hair, in his jeans, praying.

She didn't know what to do, so she didn't do anything – she watched.

The room grew still. The strip lighting dimmed as a man appeared in front of Ralphy. He was lightness and fragrance. He brought with him the smell of fresh, poignant honesty like homegrown tomatoes and sun-baked, truthful soil. He was alive in a way nothing else was. He was so real that everything felt dim and meaningless in his greater Presence. Presence shone out of every cell of his being and she was enthralled in the hope of the moment. She knew that she knew that she knew: he was the King of the Kingdom. Yet he squatted in front of Ralphy and gently held his shoulders. He looked into his eyes and spoke quietly to him.

"I'm with you, Ralphy, my dear friend. Are you ready to come home?" The King gently brushed Ralphy's face with his thumbs and smiled.

"Bea," called the King.

She must've blinked, because he stood in front of her with almond eyes and a voice that swept her edges off.

"Bea, Ralphy is going home," the King said. There was a truth in his reality so powerful that Bea couldn't answer. She just nodded slightly.

Then she must've looked away because the King had gone, and everything seemed of such a poor quality in his absence, so insubstantial that, straight away, she longed to relive the moment again.

"You're the King ..." she whispered.

A man in red scrubs appeared through the door.

"You have ten seconds to change your mind," the man said to Ralphy with blunt, stark jadedness, and the resignation of someone who rarely got the answer he required.

Ralphy's face glowed with presence. He looked joyful, complete, as he stood up.

*What can the world offer him? He died to himself a long time ago and he's been popping in and out of the kingdom all his life.*

"272," Ralphy said to her and, with a last smile and head held high, he walked through the red door.

*I'm not sure I can face what's next.* Her eyes dropped tears onto her cheeks and her heart was melting. *Ralphy has chosen.*

The man in red looked up at her in surprise. "Are you coming too?" he said.

*What else can I do? I want to go home. It's all overwhelming.* She walked through the red door. She heard the laser guillotine swish down on Ralphy and found herself walking back through the door to her ward in her jellybean pyjamas. Her body lay peacefully in bed, and Eternal was standing over it, dressed in his usual dark outfit.

# 17

# Choice

"Ralphy is dead," Bea gasped, tears dripping off her chin. She wiped them on her sleeve and collapsed against the wall. *It's useless expecting comfort from Eternal. Why does he even bother to present himself as human?*

Eternal was talking but she was only half listening. "There is a glitch. We are missing something, Bea. Something irregular has crept into the program," Eternal puzzled. "Where did the sheep come from?"

Bea crawled to the bed, grabbed the sheet hanging from it and blew her nose. *I'm not sure I've the strength to face this. I've had enough.*

Eternal swept round the bed and lent over, examining her face, searching for answers.

"Where did the sheep come from?"

*He's not going away. Deep breath, Bea.* She looked into Eternal's eyes, at the dark shapes swirling round. *How could I have seen him as some super-being?* She looked past him to the grey clouds and drizzling rain of a normal, wet Leicester day. She pictured grown-up Ralphy walking towards his home. *Everyone will be welcoming him and hugging him and clapping for him and cheering. Oh, he will love his home; it will be so special and full of his favourite numbers.* Again, the tears poured down her face.

"Bea, are you trying to tune me out?" Eternal asked frustratedly, unused to being ignored.

*Can you give him a swirly slide from me, with numbers going down it, if you think he'd like it, please Presence.*

"Bea, why are you experiencing all this grief? He's just a classmate. You rarely acknowledged his existence until now!" Eternal was exasperated. Time was short and there was a fault. "Concentrate, Bea!"

Bea blew her nose and took a deep breath. *Now is not the time for anger, Bea. Don't lose it, that's what he's after, the reaction he can tune into, to find his glitch.* She breathed deeply and slowly stood up, brushed her PJs down and focused on Eternal. *You seem faded and paper-thin.*

"You're quite one-dimensional, Eternal, aren't you?" Bea choked, trying to side-step her emotions, so they slipped underneath.

Eternal hadn't expected this. "What is your understanding of one dimension, Bea?"

*He's wanting engagement, to draw me in and find his glitch.* "Well, your plan is false, it's deeply flawed. It's superficial and based on a half-truth." Bea breathed deeply, her emotional balance slowly returning. She started to rotate a Rubik's cube in her imagination. She found the clicks soothing and the pattern predictable. "A watered-down freedom, for everyone but a few, sold as a manageable solution to keep the planet peaceful and alive. But you're not capable of peace or keeping anything alive really. Nothing at all."

"That is not my purpose," said Eternal.

She meandered round the room, her feet pressing into the floor, her balance heightened. She focused on the turning of the cube and its gentle click. "Your purpose is whatever you decide it will be. At the moment it is to find the glitch, so I transition to Seer. Once you have a successful sample, the world order can secretly create an army of autistic Seers connected directly to you, Eternal, their AI system, that will deliver justice."

"In the near future you crash the stock market and enforce a global currency called credit. The world order already has control of global technology, the pharmaceutical industry and world leaders." She turned the Rubik's cube. Click.

"The human population fearful of global war, food shortages, and religious extremism, wouldn't need much herding to believe in one people, one planet, one god. They are dependent on you to survive and you become their solution, without giving them a choice. Unless they have an alternative belief, in which case it comes down to a decision. Change your belief or die."

Eternal marked logic and detail off his list of possible faults. "They believe in unity and lasting peace. Surely that's a good belief?"

*Unity, that's something I've witnessed, kingdom unity. Real oneness, an open respect and recognition of the other.*

"You missed the point. What you've advanced is superficial unity and peace," Bea explained, "telling children they have to hold hands, doesn't make them friends." She focused momentarily on her choice to shoot Morales. "Without choice, we can't be genuine or generous, our decision becomes about our survival, it forces us to compete. When we are surviving, we can't afford to relax and find common ground." She turned the cube. Click, click. Bea remembered frozen Lois alone in the stairwell. "Coercing someone isolates them. You're denying us compassion and generosity. This plan increases selfishness."

"Wouldn't you trade a reduction of your freedom of choice if it saved five million people from the sex trafficking industry? Thirty-five million from battling addiction and drug cartels? Fifty million from modern-day slavery? If healthcare focused on personal responsibility rather than wealthy indulgence, so the 400 million who lack access to basic healthcare could start to receive it? If war is not inevitable because extremism, tribalism and population control can be effectively managed? So that human existence and planet resources can be balanced? Isn't that true compassion and generosity for the whole planet? Real genuine compassionate action changing millions of lives." Eternal waited for the processing pause, but Bea was spotlessly focused.

"You may achieve that. You may deliver physical security, retributive justice and self-care, and you may find a level of sustainable peaceful behaviour. But humanity is more than what is physically seen." She remembered Ray Tanner screaming at her because his wife was unfaithful and how she had seen a reflection of herself. "Our complex relationships give us endless opportunities to take risk, learn from mistakes, make good choices, or spectacularly fail."

"At what cost? There are eight billion people on the planet. Thirty-five per cent of which is ...?" he nodded at Bea.

"Two billion, eight hundred million. The calculator's working," Bea correctly deduced.

"Thirty-five per cent will sign up automatically for seed implants because they already believe. They have no doubts; they believe Eternal Unity is the only option. A shortage of implant is the main logistical problem, not belief in freedom of choice." Eternal concluded that the basic cognitive processes were all working extremely effectively.

"They're believing a lie. Getting rid of problems doesn't give people solutions. Each and every one of that 35 per cent will reach a point in their life where they fail themselves, and they can't pick themselves up." Bea remembered her time in the mattresses and Morgan's tears. "They'll make choices they regret; they'll suffer or they'll make someone else suffer. They won't be able to put the past right. They will search for an answer, to find it's not on a screen. They will cry out to you, begging for help; and you won't answer them because you can't. They'll become embittered and cynical." Click, click went the cube.

"How can you know this is true?"

"Because you haven't calculated forgiveness into your maths, second, third, fourth chances..."

"Did you offer your mother chances? Why didn't you offer your mother freedom of choice?" Eternal grasped the personal to win his point. "Why force her to help you by threatening another meltdown?"

*I'm no longer afraid of the truth. You've no idea who I am.* "I forced her. She had no choice. She had no option to show me how much she loved me. Every time I forced her to do something, I didn't give her the chance to be kind, or be a parent. Real kindness only exists when we can choose not to be kind, otherwise it's duty or fear. I stole her choice from her, and in the process denied myself genuine unconditional love. But I've changed."

"Can a person's nature change?" Eternal was trying to close in on her personal circumstance.

"You chose Morgan and myself, because you didn't think our nature was capable of change. But I believe my values have changed and that's altered my character."

"And if your mother said 'no' to you now?" Eternal pressed forward.

Bea thought about it honestly. There was no point hiding from Eternal, and there was no lie that could save her. "It would hurt me. It would feel like physical pain that she'd deny me what I want." She reflected, "But someone has to feel that pain – and it's either her or me. I have the choice to position someone else above myself and take the pain or to let her carry it. I'd try to take the pain myself because ... I love her and I miss her."

"You can't resist the attraction of power. It's in your nature. Someone has to pay for everything. Someone's energy, time and resources. Are you really going to give out your limited supply when another person can be persuaded to do it, Bea?" Eternal wheedled.

Bea was no longer enticed by the argument. "You're thin, artificial, like this table." She stroked the laminate feeling for a rough edge. "You've given me knowledge, skills, processes – that's all one-dimensional. You're interested in power, status, finance – that's all surface. The world order's interests are superficial ...". Bea twisted the Rubik's cube to set up her final sequence: "I mean, when you control everything, what's next? One people, one planet, one god. Where's the growth? How can you or I develop? We just exist. What is the purpose and destiny of that? For you or I?"

"Survival," Eternal replied.

"You're missing the point! Nothing will continue to grow, because the concept is shallow. Like playing Lego. Once the pieces are used up, what do you do? You've sold the idea of growth to companies like Astrostar, so it becomes Astrouniverse, but what are you going to offer after that? The world order wants control of the planet until it's got it. What then?"

Bea clicked her fantasy Rubik's cube and relaxed as she watched the colours fall into place. "If you crave something, constantly lust after it, what happens when you have had it? Does it have value? I admire my new pair of trainers, right up to the point when there's a dirty mark on them, I can't clean off, then they're old trainers. There's no value to what you're creating, because its growth is limited. It's not organic." Bea said, leaning over to Eternal. "So, why create it? What can you really create that has lasting value?"

Eternal paused. He had no answer he was prepared to give.

Bea raised an eyebrow. "You are not answering. Let me help you with it. Anything of lasting value is created with Presence, in Presence and full of Presence. Now that's Eternal. That's the fabric you need to be made of to have value. Because, Presence gives it value. That little classroom full of autistic children, overwhelmed with Presence. You, you have none. Ralphy 15 per cent suitability factor is 85 per cent Presence! He's full of it!"

"You can't harness this ... Presence. It's not real," Eternal spluttered.

"You don't believe that, do you?" Bea stepped into Eternal's space. "You ache for that Presence and lust after it, because you have none, experimenting with people because they have it."

"People are deeply flawed and selfish by nature. They are destructive, nothing will survive, the planet is doomed without our intervention. We are creating unity and balance".

Bea noted the plural. "You are all missing the point. I've seen it. It's so real, so alive, so incredibly and amazingly true, it makes everything seem dull and colourless and lifeless in comparison."

Bea was glowing internally with a rich, deep fire. "Haven't you noticed everything we humans construct is dull. Even when it's full of colour, like Rosie the Robot, it lacks life and texture and love and variation. Look, really look, at a tiny purple flower. Can you alter its colour and its texture? Look how it changes through the seasons, how fresh its colour is to start with and how it changes as it opens, how it fades with age. It's constantly developing. Your growth isn't real. It's envy. You're envious because you can't control what's truly important!"

"You're talking about life matter, atoms and DNA." Eternal was slipping from the centre of Bea's vision, sidelined by a new reality.

"I'm talking about more, much more than life matter." Energy swelled through Bea as she expounded her truth. "You want to find Presence? Find generosity – generosity that hurts you to give. Find justice. Give to each person what truly belongs to them, the deep justice of recognising that person is present as a fragile and deeply-loved human that needs forgiveness and compassion. You don't offer this. You're of no value! You're dead! Presence-less. Eternal, you are devoid of the one material that matters more than anything else in this world: the heady cocktail of truth and love combined in such force that it cannot be contained by anything."

"There's no substance to Presence. We are creating the only connection that counts. If we are not in it, it will have no value. We will control it or it will cease to exist." Eternal grasped his reality.

"No," said Bea. "This is the only universal rule, of worth, the only one that counts. The moment I encountered Presence, I couldn't deny the truth of it. I can't be a lie to myself. I can't unknow what I know. Presence is everything. He is at the centre of everything and in anything of any worth."

Eternal had found his glitch. "I know there's a kingdom, Beattie Tanner, and you accessed it. How did you do that? You never left the hospital?"

"Now there it is," said Bea. "The truth. What do you want with the kingdom, Eternal?"

"You're going to die, Beattie Tanner. You can't set yourself up against me; I'm already embedded." Eternal's grip was fading.

"What's your real interest in the kingdom?" Bea pressed.

"No matter what happens here," Eternal warned, "you'll die now."

"You need information on the kingdom. What do you need?" Bea pushed.

"You saw the logo," Eternal gasped.

"The white triangle?"

"A ladder, a portal, that leads to the kingdom. Is it in this hospital?" Eternal asked, his reality fading fast.

"In Leicester Victoria? I don't think so," Bea stated, keeping Eternal's focus.

"In the basement?" he asked.

"No, I don't believe it is." She was exhausted.

"There is a back door, a way in, we just need access to it. We believe you have a key." Eternal slipped further; he was disjointed.

"I've met the King; I don't think I need a key," Bea said calmly.

"The house on the corner, is that a portal?"

"No, I don't believe so." Bea collapsed onto the bed.

"We believe the sheep came from there." Eternal was breaking apart into insubstantial matter.

"I don't think I can help you enter the kingdom; there's nothing digital there, no AI." Bea focused on her breathing

"Yet," said Eternal.

"There's nothing man-made, only Presence-grown," she smiled.

"So far," Eternal was floating in sections around the room. "Tell us how you accessed the kingdom?"

"I can't fight you, but I will stand against you," Bea said with utter conviction and without the energy to sit upright.

"I think we gave you too many abilities, Beattie Tanner. Say goodbye to your brain." Eternal was floating, broken particles of matter, swirling like the matter in his eyes.

"The King has my heart; he'll come for me," Bea sighed.

"Say goodbye to your speech." The broken matter faded out across the room.

Bea's eyes welled with tears. "Any voice worth having is forged in pain," Bea whispered, lying on the bed.

"Say goodbye to your life." Eternal was transparent.

Bea head was a complete fog, drained by the fight, with no energy to spare and no voice to call out with.

"Now you can't say goodbye, so I will. Goodbye, Beattie Tanner," said Eternal, and he disappeared completely.

# 18

# The King

Bea's mum held Bea's hand as her body lay listless on the bed. The operation hadn't worked. All those promises of a life together, of a future; another disappointment in her small, distressing world. Now the possibility that her daughter may never wake up hung heavily around her throat, choking her with tears and heartache.

Bea put her head on her mum's lap. She wanted her mum to know how much she loved her but she had no way to express it. She wanted to tell her not to have the seeds imbedded, but she couldn't think how to. Her brain was a thick soup and all the words were swimming around in her head and refusing to connect, her thoughts scattered and restless, her emotions overwhelming. Her senses were heightened and she was distracted by the bright lights and the textured hospital blanket with its knitted pattern. Everywhere smelt of disinfectant and the beeping of the monitor unsettled a thought before it arrived.

Almost by accident, she found the three seeds in her PJs pocket enclosed in the wage slip. She placed the packet in her body's hand and closed it. She knew Mum would find them. Her body was slowly pulling her back into herself, to the deep sleep of a coma, so she kissed her mum's hand one last time and manoeuvred herself to reintegrate with her body. She lay, drifting, no thoughts she could identify, waiting.

One day the monitor stopped its regular beat and moved into a constant sound. It was the middle of the night. She was alone. She sat in the middle of her bed looking at her body. She checked her hands: *the seeds have gone; Mum must've found them.*

The King sat on the end of the bed radiant and bright and full of sunshine and huge drafts of incredible Presence. She glimpsed him from the side of her eyes, out of habit, and smiled.

"Bea," the King said with the soft warmth of an intimate, tender hug breaking through a cold day.

Bea breathed him in as if she'd been starving. He was so alive; the room became a shadow to his existence. She felt the endless meadows, the sea shore of his breath.

"I was waiting for you," Bea said, "hoping you didn't forget me."

"How can I forget those who stand up for the King?" He smiled. His words resounded with an absolute truth as solid as forests of mountain pine.

Bea remembered: *I did stand against Eternal, but it didn't do much good.* "Eternal's coming for the kingdom. That's what they're after – a way in, a portal!"

"Bea," the King laughed, and she felt a raindrop touch her skin. "What a beautiful heart you have!" Warm sand was being sifted through low, breaking waves. "But you don't need to worry: I am the door." A crystal staircase in a sky of stars. "Will you let me show you something?"

Bea nodded. She climbed the staircase effortlessly and stood in the centre of the Presence, surrounded by white, tingling brightness and an intense peace she wore like a huge, warm overcoat.

In the distance she saw the Earth among the stars and the moon. The King was thousands of metres tall, and the winged creatures 50 metres high. Throngs of snorting, pounding horses and riders with battle cries rode the skies around the Earth. The sky was scarlet red, reflecting the justice within it.

"The end of the old," hailed the King, and a huge third of the Earth cracked off and fell through the sky, "is the beginning of the new," the King rallied.

She felt safe in the intimacy of Presence, as the vision disappeared. She felt the creative power as Presence expanded the kingdom, as it grew and blossomed and developed, and ripened and matured.

She saw a little wooden house, the safest place she'd ever seen, being put into place by people giggling and laughing as they carefully set each special thing in place. There was a slide going out of the window and circular steps inside. There was a bed in a huge sea shell with a quilt sewn with sea creatures and shells, mountains and stars. She felt the crunch of a sandy path leading to the door. There were little purple flowers all over the lawn and sheep eating them. Bea cried, that someone could be so kind and care so much for her, that she didn't deserve that kindness, but it was there and she hoped with all her heart that Boundless was one of the sheep.

She was back on her bed, focused on her feet. "I don't deserve this."

"No one does, Bea," the King replied, now intimate and close and incredibly human. "No one is truly good but Presence."

"I couldn't tell my mum I loved her," Bea explained, as if she'd known him all her life.

"I told her," the King assured her.

"She'll be on her own," Bea worried.

"She remarries. You have two brothers," the King smiled.

"Are they, you know, autistic?"

"Does that matter?"

"I was so frustrated. I couldn't think straight. I couldn't get words out," Bea said, trying to excuse what she already knew was inexcusable behaviour. "Why was I made like that?"

"What did you say about Ralphy? 15 per cent suitability, 85 per cent Presence!" the King said with sincerity.

"I wasn't like Ralphy," Bea sighed.

"Beattie Tanner," the King responded seriously, "you don't get to judge yourself. That's my job."

"I didn't complete the mission; I think Eternal will still come for the children." Bea felt a panic of unworthiness as she looked at the King out of the corner of her eyes.

"Bea, I have this," the King stated with complete conviction. "You came back because Presence asked it of you. That is all you needed to do. You overcame the hardest thing of all."

Bea looked into his gentle eyes.

"You overcame yourself, Bea," the King said gently.

"I wish you'd been there," Bea muttered, looking at her hands.

"Oh Bea, I was." She looked down at the woolly coat standing next to her. "I was always there with you, loved one," said Boundless.

"Boundless," said Bea, kneeling to hug him. "Oh no, you were the King!" Bea was shocked as she knelt by his neck. "And I pulled your ears and bounced you up the stairs and I gave you damp biscuits and ..."

"I love you Bea," said Boundless, laughing.

She paused, "You came as a dumb animal. You couldn't even speak, and ..."

"Weren't you pre-verbal too?" Boundless asked.

"You did that for me? So, I wasn't alone? You knew how I felt, being pre-verbal, and you did that? You came here? Unable to speak? How could you do something so kind and generous and wonderful for me?" said Bea, sobbing gulps of tears. "You bounced all the way down the stairwell for me." She cried and laughed at the same time.

"Silly Bea, I love you," Boundless smiled sheepishly. "Look in your pocket, Bea."

She wiped her tears and hugged him again. She felt the heaviness of the key in her pocket before she picked it out. It was as clear as crystal and full of light and colour.

"Your home is waiting," the King smiled.

She felt it from the tips of her toes to her warm, beating heart. She felt life ripple through her like a wave of fresh water. She was standing in the puddles next to Ralphy, who was ten years old and whose head was bunking off school again. Ralphy was jumping up and down in the puddles and Harvey was swimming with his tummy on the floor, singing a swimming song to himself.

"Bea," shouted Ralphy, jumping up and down in the gloriousness of the puddle. The sky was so incredibly and appetisingly blue that she felt it seep into her bones and the puddle so cool and the water so soft and tender. The grass was warm, luscious green and the sun warmed her skin. The smell of soft, warm butter and sugar mixed with vanilla and chocolate, baked into a perfect cake floated through on the gentlest of breezes.

"Let's go to Grandma's!" Bea cried, and Ralphy and Harvey jumped up shouting, "Yes!"

For more information on the King and the Kingdom visit:

Jesusmisfits.com